"You Know I Want You," Lance Murmured. "You Have To Be The Sexiest Woman I've Ever Known."

"But we want different things," he continued. "This isn't a game. We'll be going our separate ways in a day or two. I don't want—"

Marcy placed a finger against his lips.

"I know all that. But *I* don't want a long-term relationship. I'm not saying I fall into bed with every man who makes me feel special. But you have to admit there is something out of the ordinary between us, and we need to explore what that is before it's too late."

Leaning in, she placed a light kiss on his lips. "Please, Lance. Please let us find out if this is really magic. Give me a chance."

The fire crackled as the sparks he'd tried to bury ignited. Thin lines he'd drawn began to combust and his resolve blew away like a puff of smoke.

Dear Reader,

As expected, Silhouette Desire has loads of passionate, powerful and provocative love stories for you this month. Our DYNASTIES: THE DANFORTHS continuity is winding to a close with the penultimate title, *Terms of Surrender,* by Shirley Rogers. A long-lost Danforth heir may just have been found—and heavens, is this prominent family in for a big surprise! And talk about steamy secrets, Peggy Moreland is back with *Sins of a Tanner,* a stellar finale to her series THE TANNERS OF TEXAS.

If it's scandalous behavior you're looking for, look no farther than *For Services Rendered* by Anne Marie Winston. This MANTALK book—the series that offers stories strictly from the hero's point of view—has a fabulous hero who does the heroine a very special favor. Hmmmm. And Alexandra Sellers is back in Desire with a fresh installment of her SONS OF THE DESERT series. *Sheikh's Castaway* will give you plenty of sweet (and naughty) dreams.

Even more shocking situations pop up in Linda Conrad's sensual *Between Strangers.* Imagine if you were stuck on the side of the road during a blizzard and a sexy cowboy offered *you* shelter from the storm…. (Hello, are you still with me?) Rounding out the month is Margaret Allison's *Principles and Pleasures,* a daring romp between a workaholic heroine and a man she doesn't know is actually her archenemy.

So settle in for some sensual, scandalous love stories…and enjoy every moment!

Melissa Jeglinski

Melissa Jeglinski
Senior Editor, Silhouette Desire

Please address questions and book requests to:
Silhouette Reader Service
U.S.: 3010 Walden Ave., P.O. Box 1325, Buffalo, NY 14269
Canadian: P.O. Box 609, Fort Erie, Ont. L2A 5X3

Between Strangers

LINDA CONRAD

Silhouette® Desire

Published by Silhouette Books

America's Publisher of Contemporary Romance

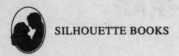 **SILHOUETTE BOOKS**

ISBN 0-373-76619-X

BETWEEN STRANGERS

Visit Silhouette Books at www.eHarlequin.com

Printed in U.S.A.

Books by Linda Conrad

Silhouette Desire

The Cowboy's Baby Surprise #1446
Desperado Dad #1458
Secrets, Lies...and Passion #1470
*The Gentrys: Cinco #1508
*The Gentrys: Abby #1516
*The Gentrys: Cal #1524
Slow Dancing with a Texan #1577
The Laws of Passion #1609
Between Strangers #1619

*The Gentrys

LINDA CONRAD

Born in Brazil to a commercial pilot and his wife, Linda Conrad was raised in south Florida and has been a dreamer and storyteller for as long as she can remember. After her mother's death a few years ago, she moved from her then-home in Texas to Southern California and gave up her previous life as a stockbroker to rededicate herself to her first love—writing.

Linda and her husband, along with a Siamese-mix cat named Sam, recently moved back to south Florida. She's been writing contemporary romances for about five years and loves sharing them with readers. She enjoys growing roses, reading cozy mysteries and sexy romances and driving her little convertible in the sunshine. But most important, Linda loves learning about—and living with—passion.

It makes Linda's day to hear from readers. Visit with her at www.LindaConrad.com.

To Alice Zyne,
who's become the mother of my heart.
Thanks for taking me into the family
and for believing in me!

One

Unbelievable. It looked as if driving the next twenty miles to the State Line Truckstop was going to take more than three hours.

Or rather, it would take that long *if* he didn't get stuck in a snowdrift, and *if* the state police hadn't closed all the side roads the same way they'd done with the interstate.

Lance White Eagle Steele jacked up the heater in his newly purchased four-wheel-drive SUV, wishing for a thermos of hot coffee. He'd been so sure this two-lane road would be a good shortcut, getting him around a major section of snow-closed interstate highway. It had never occurred to him that it might take six times longer to navigate the icy backcountry roads through what had turned into a blinding blizzard.

Well, at least he was on his way home. Thinking of the ranch and the warmth of the people waiting there for his return, he realized that another few hours or an extra day wouldn't matter much. He would still be able to make it back to Montana in time for the annual Christmas Eve party.

For a few frustrating moments back there at O'Hare, Lance had worried that he would be forced to miss Christmas on the ranch altogether. His bad timing was perfect. He'd come in from New Orleans and planned to make a connecting flight to Great Falls. Only, just as he'd arrived, all flights had been canceled due to the midwinter snowstorm.

The bad news hadn't stopped there. The entire upper Midwest was socked in and, according to weather forecasts, flights might continue to be delayed for days. Three waves of low-pressure systems were chasing each other, barreling across the skies and burying the Great Plains in mountains of snow.

The crowds at O'Hare had begun to bed down on the floors, expecting to be stuck there for some time. But Lance had been determined to get home for that party.

Patting his leather winter jacket at a spot above his breast pocket, he was heartened by the solid feel of the ring box he carried. Everything would be okay. He just knew it. Soon his whole life would be headed down the right course, just as he was now headed down the right roads to get himself home.

It had been a fairly simple matter to convince the rental car agent to sell him a slightly used SUV so he could get out of the overcrowded airport and be on his way home. Good references and a really high credit line on his card worked wonders toward convincing the man that his paperwork for the sale could be faxed the week after next when government offices reopened after the holidays.

Lance squinted out the windshield as the snowfall worsened, blocking his view of the poorly lit road ahead. He turned on the wipers, rubbed at the foggy glass and did his best. This was turning out to be one of the worst snowstorms he'd ever seen. And in ten years of traveling the rodeo circuits throughout the American West, he'd seen quite a few.

Using the edge of his hand, he swiped another path across the inside of the fogged glass in front of him. The defroster and heater were working overtime, and Lance gave a silent prayer of thanks for being inside and warm instead of out there in the bitter December wind.

He cleared enough of a spot to see just in time... giving him a last second opportunity to swerve and avoid hitting a bulky dark shape at the side of the road.

"Damn," he grumbled while he guided his wheels toward the other lane.

As his car skidded past, the dark form became a human being hunched against the wind and carrying an oversize load wrapped in a blanket. Checking his rearview mirror, Lance spotted the outlined shadow of a car at the side of the road a few yards back and figured the guy must have broken down.

Poor bastard would soon freeze to death out here. Talk about bad luck. Lance had been driving these back roads for six hours now and hadn't run into a single soul who was stupid enough to be out in such a blizzard.

As much as he needed to keep going, Lance certainly couldn't leave a fellow traveler stranded on a deserted country road in this weather. During emergencies, people had to stick together for survival. If he'd been stuck, he would hope someone would have stopped to help.

Lance was pretty handy at car repairs, maybe he could help the guy get his car going. And maybe it wouldn't take too long for him to be on his way home again.

Stopping in the road, but leaving the engine running, Lance opened the car door and stepped out onto the highway. A strong gust of Arctic wind blasted him as ice crunched under his boots. He hung on to his Stetson and tried to peer through the blowing snow while he fought his way back to the stranded motorist.

Through the haze of snow flurries and sleet, he managed a clearer glimpse of the person coming toward him. Lance was stunned to realize it was a woman.

Her head was covered by a thin scarf made of some drab-colored material. And she was burdened down with an oversize bundle that she'd covered with an old army blanket.

She came closer and after another second he finally caught his first glimpse of her eyes. They were light brown and a little overly bright in the low light of the snowstorm. Her face was thin and her lips were pursed with the effort to breathe.

Her clothes were covered with snow and getting wetter by the minute. While her face was devoid of makeup, her skin was smooth and what hair he could see looked like a fine golden halo around her face. She looked like an angel in distress.

The woman must be totally insane to be out here alone in this storm. Or maybe she was on drugs. He figured he'd better watch his step with her.

"What's wrong with your car?" he yelled over the howling wind.

She was still breathing hard from the exertion of walking against the wind while carrying the heavy-looking bundle. Her every gasp was outlined in the crystallized air.

"I'm afraid it's done for," she wheezed. "I know there's plenty of gas, and I just had the battery charged at a gas station in Minneapolis. But it stopped dead in the middle of the road. And after I coasted to the side, the engine refused to turn over again. Nothing happens when I crank the key. Absolutely nothing."

"Get in my car before you freeze to death out here," he shouted. "I'll take a look at it. Give me your keys."

As she came nearer, the woman's eyes became wary, hesitant. "I have…" she gulped as she handed over the car keys and held up her burden.

Heaven help her, he muttered under his breath. Whatever she had with her wasn't worth her life. Why didn't she just set the thing down somewhere and come back for it later?

He skated back to the SUV he'd left idling in the

middle of the deserted road and ripped open the back door. ''Throw it in the back seat and get the hell inside now!''

She tossed him a quick, glaring look and shook her head. ''I have to keep her close to my body until she warms up some.'' As she unwrapped a tiny edge of the blanket to show him, he saw the top of a woolly baby's cap that was almost covering curly blond hair.

Lance nearly lost his footing altogether as he raced to help the woman get herself and her child into the front seat by the heater. Whatever in the world would possess a woman to take a kid out in such a storm?

Though a little frightened and somewhat hesitant to accept help from a complete stranger, Marcy Griffin had no choice but to climb into the front seat of the cowboy's SUV. Another fifteen minutes in this cold and the baby might've gotten chilled through and be on her way to pneumonia.

It was a terrible decision to have to make: risk getting involved with a stranger who could be a crazed maniac, or take a chance on the life and health of her precious daughter. Actually, there hadn't been much of a choice.

The man wearing the cowboy hat had shut the car doors to keep the interior warm and then headed back through the storm to look at her car. Marcy looked down at the child in her arms and found that her baby was still sleeping soundly.

It would be just as well if Angie slept right through this ordeal. Marcy knew her child was hungry, cold and tired, and she wished with all her might that things could be different, for her daughter's sake.

But at least the two of them were still alive. And one way or another, they were headed toward a better life. That was the most important thing right now.

Ten minutes later, just as Marcy was beginning to feel her fingers and toes again, the cowboy opened the rear passenger door and began installing Angie's car seat.

"You were right," he told her. "Your car is a goner. I think you must've cracked the block."

"If we're going to ride with you, can you get Angie's things out of my trunk, please?"

"Things?"

"Diapers, baby food, bottles…" Marcy couldn't see his expression under the brim of the hat, but she imagined he was scowling at his bad luck, stopping for such high-maintenance passengers.

"I'll get them moved over," he muttered. "You make sure the baby's seat is secure and get her loaded in. I'll be right back."

She scrambled out and made short work of getting Angie buckled into her seat. Angie shifted around and nestled down in the familiar form-fitting cocoon but never opened her eyes. She'd been so quiet for so long that Marcy put her cheek against the child's forehead, hoping to find that nothing was seriously wrong with her. Thankfully, Angie's temperature seemed fine.

There was no third seat in the SUV and it didn't take the cowboy long to fill up the cargo space with their things. Once they were all buckled in and cautiously on their way, Marcy closed her eyes and gave a silent prayer of thanks for their rescue.

Peeking out through half-closed lids to check on the stranger who'd picked them up, she decided to thank him for being their hero *only* when they were safe and sound and she was sure he wasn't really a serial killer. Marcy studied his profile while he concentrated on the slick road.

What kind of man was this?

He'd pushed the hat back on his forehead so he could get a better view out the windshield. She remembered thinking how tall and broad-shouldered he was as they'd been standing out on the side of the road.

Now she could see that he was also powerfully built. He had what could only be described as a commanding presence. Just by breathing, he seemed to suck up all the oxygen and space surrounding his body, and Marcy could imagine him as a leader of troops. A man others would respect.

Thank heaven. Perhaps they would all get out of this storm safely.

Looking closer, she noted the jet-black, slightly too long hair under his gray cowboy hat…and quickly scanned the rugged angles and jutting jawline of his face. The lighting wasn't very good, but his bronzed skin, high cheekbones and Roman nose all looked Native American.

Which was why the first thing out of his mouth surprised her so much.

"The name's Lance Steele," he said without looking directly at her. "What'll I call you?"

"Oh, please excuse me. Things have been so…" She caught herself and began again. "My name's Marcy Griffin. And my baby is Angelina…. 'Angie' most of the time unless I'm frustrated and trying to get her attention." In her daughter's entire nine months of life, Marcy hadn't come that close to apologizing for simply being alive—the way she would've done in her best-forgotten past.

She had no intention of ever allowing herself to become such a wimp again.

The corner of his mouth cracked slightly but not enough to actually call it a smile. "Is the kid…Angie…okay? She's not sick, is she?"

"She's fine. It's just been a long, hard day for her."

"Where are you two headed? And what the devil were you thinking to bring a child out in a—" He screwed up his mouth and looked as if he was about to spew a raft of curse words at her.

After he breathed deeply and rolled his shoulders for a second or two, he seemed a little more in control. "Sorry. But you two should be someplace dry and warm right now. Not out becoming stranded in one of the worst blizzards in history. Where's your husband? What will he have to say when he finds out how much danger you two were in?"

The flash of a reminder about Mike made her forget to be careful and thoughtful before she answered the questions of a cowboy who had yet to completely prove he wasn't a maniac. "If my ex-husband cared one way or the other about being a father in the first place…or if he'd ever bothered to meet the baby he helped to create…I'm sure he would have nothing good to say about anything I did.''

She folded her arms across her chest and stared out at the inhospitable landscape. Well, that little speech was more than she'd said to anyone in months. And it had been much more venomous than was strictly necessary. She had better find a less combative way to get to know their rescuer.

''I'm sorry,'' she said with a sigh. ''I realize you don't know anything about my divorce. Angie and I are on our own. I'm trying to get to a new job. It's really a great opportunity. But we have to be there by the first of January. I thought we had lots of time, but…''

''How far away is this new job?'' he interrupted.

''Not that far, under normal circumstances. Cheyenne…in Wyoming.''

''Yeah, I know where it is. I've spent a lot of time in Cheyenne.''

''Is that your home? You aren't headed there now, are you?''

The slight shake of his head was almost imperceptible. ''Nope. I'm headed for a ranch outside Great Falls. That's my home.''

He'd said the word *home* with such obvious reverence, she just knew some lucky woman must be waiting there for his return. Marcy didn't think she'd better question him any further right now, however, especially on the subject of who he was fighting his way home to see.

Out of nowhere, a loud cracking sound split through the piercing noise of the howling winds.

Lance slowly put his foot on the brake and the SUV came to a sliding stop...within a foot of a huge pine tree that had landed across the road directly in their path.

Both of them sat in stunned silence, looking out the windshield at nothing but pine needles and bark in every direction. There was total quiet for what seemed like a half hour, but it was probably only a few seconds.

"Stay put. I'll go move it out of the way," Lance growled.

"Is it the whole tree?"

He shook his head in frustration. "It's just a damned big branch. I'll handle it." He got out and slammed the door behind him.

He knew he shouldn't take his frustrations out on a perfect stranger. None of this was her fault. Whether she was in the SUV or not hadn't caused the wind to take off the biggest branch he'd ever seen and lay it end to end blocking the road.

Okay, so there was nothing he'd like better than to never have seen her and her baby standing by the roadside in the first place. He had a timetable of his own and no time to deal with someone else's problems.

But that little outburst of hers about the no-good scum of a husband abandoning them both before the baby was even born had made him furious. He'd known plenty of bums like that from his rodeo days. Men who would play around with women and then disappear when things got serious.

But knowing about it didn't make hearing the truth from the woman's side any easier. It was despicable. The thought of having a family right in the palm of your hand and casually tossing it aside rather than cherishing every minute made him angry and itching to hit something.

Nothing on earth would make him abandon these two to the storm. He didn't know why he'd been hapless enough to be saddled with them, but it looked as if fate had stepped in yet again and changed his plans. At the very least, he would take them to a truck stop and make sure they were safe.

Pulling his hat lower and hunching down inside his jacket, Lance stepped out of the warmth of the running car and into a polar blast of Arctic air. The temperature must've dropped twenty degrees in the past hour.

He tried not to breathe too deeply in the sharp raw cold, knowing all too well how his lungs would burn if he did. A man couldn't be a wrangler on a ranch in northern Montana without being fully aware of all the dangers lurking in the long, hard winters there.

By the time he made it around the hood through the blinding, blowing snow to the downed tree branch, he felt the bone-chilling cold penetrating all the way down to his internal organs. He quickly discovered that the pine branch was lying across the entire two lanes, making it impossible for the SUV to go around. The limb was thick, full of bushy needles and loaded with heavy snow.

There was nothing to do but drag it out of the way. But two major tugs against the full weight of the branch told him moving it by hand was out of the question. Man, what he'd give for a cross-cut saw just about now.

"Can I help?" Marcy's question grabbed his attention.

"I told you to stay put," he yelled against the wind. "The temperature out here has dropped beyond dangerous. Get back in the car."

"You'll never move anything that heavy by yourself," she said, ignoring his question in a voice raised above the roar of the storm. "Can we use the SUV to push it out of the way?"

"No." But her question gave him an idea.

Before buying the SUV, when he'd been checking out the compartment that held the spare tire, he was a little surprised to find jumper cables, a fold-up metal shovel, a cable-size rope and a thick blanket all stuffed in around the spare. The rental agent told him it was standard procedure to keep emergency supplies like those in every car they rented out during the dead of winter.

"That'll have to work," he grumbled to himself as he stomped to the cargo compartment of the SUV.

By the time he'd retrieved the rope from the compartment, Marcy was beside him again. "What're you going to do?"

"We can't push it out of the way. But maybe we can pull it aside far enough to drive around," he told her.

Like most newer cars and trucks, this one didn't have decent steel bumpers. But it did have a heavy-duty hitch installed to the frame under the rear bumper.

Lance glanced over at Marcy and caught the shiver that pulsed through her body. She wasn't dressed warmly enough for this kind of weather. That coat of hers was worn out.

There was no question which of them would do what. "Do you think you can turn the SUV around so that it's headed in the other direction? I'll attach the rope and make sure it'll hold."

"Yes…yes, of course…" she stuttered.

When she was safely in the driver's seat, he finally relaxed his shoulders. At least her feet wouldn't be subject to frostbite while inside the warm vehicle.

He stepped aside and guided her by hand movements to a point he figured would be the best for moving the branch. After he'd made sure the rope was securely tied to both tree and SUV, he waved her ahead. She cracked the driver's-side window to hear him over the wind.

She tried to inch ahead but the wheels were spinning against the icy patches and the building snow crystals. She couldn't manage to get any traction.

"Let me try it," he hollered.

Instead of scooting over the center console, Marcy hopped out of the driver's door and started around the hood to the passenger side. She raised her hands to cover her mouth against the biting cold, and he got his first good look at her gloves.

Or her utter *lack* of adequate gloves would be a truer description of what he'd seen as she dashed past. He had originally thought she'd been wearing woolen mittens. Now he was shocked to see holes where her fingers poked through the thin material. She would have frostbite for sure.

Marcy climbed inside through the other door, and he slid into the driver's seat. It didn't take him but five more minutes to rock the SUV ahead, dragging the branch out of one lane. Two more minutes and the rope was untied and crammed back in the compartment with the spare. Then he successfully managed to turn the SUV once again so they could be on their way.

He eased the SUV down the road past the bulk of the tree. Once they were clear, he slowed and put it in Park.

Turning to face her, he tried to remain calm as he said, ''Marcy, give me your hands.''

''What?'' She swiveled and blinked at his odd demand.

Holding his own hands out, palms up, he cocked his head and waited.

She tentatively started to lay her hands in his, but looked wary and confused. It was all he could do not to break down and beg her to quickly do as he'd asked. He didn't want to scare her, but this was too important.

Two

Marcy hadn't realized how difficult it might be to give up control and let Lance take her hands. She should've known. After all, it had been more than eighteen months since she'd let a man so much as touch her.

When she glanced up to check the sincerity in his midnight-black eyes, her breath caught in her throat. Was that an erotic spark she saw in those eyes? Marcy had to fight within herself to ignore it and the powerful electric current she'd felt.

Eventually she surrendered her hands to him and stared blankly at where they were joined. The contrast between the golden skin of the back of his hands and the stark whiteness of her fingers drew her entire focus.

Lance studied their hands, too, his face contorted

in a scowl. "We need to get these wet things off you in a hurry."

"Huh?" That shocking sizzle of sensual awareness she'd just felt had obviously turned her into an idiot.

He didn't wait for her to come to her senses. Tearing off her gloves, he dropped them in front of the heater. But he still didn't let go of her hands.

Wonderful. Now the jolts of electricity were shooting clear up her arms and down her spine, making her overly warm and hypersensitive to every tiny touch. And here she'd thought her fingers were numbed by the cold.

She managed to keep herself from pulling away. Not that she really wanted to. Never in her life had a man's touch affected her so strongly. Her mind froze at the same time her body heated.

But Lance's next move stirred the blood clear to her toes and drove her totally past common sense. He tenderly lifted her hands to his mouth and lightly blew a warm breath across her fingers and palms.

Fire raced from her hands up through her veins, landing with a roar in her belly. Suddenly panicked by the intimate movements and by a fever that was driving her to madness, Marcy shuddered and tugged hard against his grip.

Either her frantic jerking or her audible gasps must've broken through Lance's intense concentration. "Don't pull away. Let me warm you up."

The tone of his voice sounded more erotic to her than his words. She was already burning up simply from his touch.

"I'm concerned about frostbite," he advised sternly.

Marcy couldn't keep looking into his eyes. The intimacy was too much for her to take.

"I'm okay," she told him as she began rubbing her hands together to get the circulation back.

"Don't rub your hands that way." He reached for her hands again. "Rubbing is one of the worst things you can do for frostbite."

When their fingers touched once more, he stopped talking and she heard his sudden intake of breath. She wondered if the lightning bolt of sensation she'd felt had seared him as deeply as it had her.

She found herself looking down and away from their joined hands. Anywhere but back into his eyes.

After a too-long second of uncomfortable silence, he finally placed her hands next to the heater's fan and then let her go. "Keep your fingers in front of the blower. They may start to ache but they'll thaw more slowly that way."

Lance sat back in his seat and put the SUV into gear. "I think we should make it to a truck stop in about an hour." His voice was rough and dry. "That is, if we don't have any more emergency roadblocks to get around."

Neither of them said anything more as quiet filled the SUV, and all that could be heard was the blower on the heater's fan and the rumble of the engine as the SUV strained against the icy winds and slick roads.

Marcy couldn't find enough of her voice to say anything at all. She sat stunned in silence for long minutes, trying to figure out what had just happened between them.

Her brain slowly came back around to focusing on her surroundings at the exact moment she heard Angie begin to stir in the back seat. Relieved and grateful, she figured that her baby would be a good distraction to take her mind off the odd reaction she'd had to Lance's touch. Marcy unbuckled the seat belt and twisted around on her knees to check the little girl.

"What's the matter with your baby?" he asked. "Is she all right?"

"She's just waking up, but I'm betting she'll soon be loudly voicing her complaints."

"Complaints?"

Angie opened her eyes, and Marcy decided to slide past the center console to go between the two front seats in order to reach her. The familiar sounds of the baby's "I'm wet and hungry" cries told her that it was indeed time for a change.

"Whoa," Lance bellowed over the din created by Angie's screams and the fierce sounds of the blowing winds. "Should I stop?"

"We're barely moving as it is," Marcy told him. "I trust you. Just keep going. I can reach her diaper bag in the back," she continued. "Just let me change Angie and try giving her the water bottle. I'll wait to feed her until we can get inside someplace warm." At least, she hoped Angie could wait a little longer.

Lance concentrated on his driving. Still shaken from his crazy reaction to the touch of her skin and the spark of something he'd seen in her eyes, he now had one more thing about Marcy Griffin that deviled him.

She trusted him to keep them safe. He was frantically searching his memory for any other time when someone had actually trusted him that much. The only thing he could come up with was when Buck pulled him off the rodeo circuit and hired him to be in charge of his ranch's rodeo stock program. He must've trusted him a lot to do that. Right?

Lance had never been able to figure out what made women tick, though. And this one was turning out to be more confusing than any of the others.

Take Buck's daughter, Lorna, for instance. She was a good friend. Someone who would gladly ride across the Montana countryside with him, and someone he could also take to movies on lonely Saturday nights. Lorna was steady and predictable. And he was sure she would accept his ring. She would make him a good wife.

But never…ever…had he felt the same kind of steamy heat and staggering flood of senses that he'd experienced just by touching Marcy's hands.

He couldn't remember any time in those days before he settled down on the ranch—and certainly never with the woman who lived there now—when this intense kind of desire had bypassed his good judgment. With Lorna, he'd wanted to wait until the two of them were at least engaged before they took things past friendship. And he was sure Lorna felt the same way. Letting sex rule a relationship was not a thing he felt comfortable doing with someone who would be his life partner.

So this sudden craving to take a perfect stranger into his arms and kiss her senseless was totally unexpected and absolutely unwanted. Perhaps the life-and-death circumstances they found themselves in were making his normal male reactions to a pretty woman suddenly seem much more powerful.

He decided not to dwell on it too much. The best thing for him to do was to talk to Marcy. Try to make friends with her. Keep things casual. They probably would be together for several more hours at least. By the time he was on his way down the road without her, perhaps the two of them would've found they had nothing in common and his libido would've settled back in line.

Good plan. Now if only his body would cooperate.

Within fifteen minutes Marcy had quieted her baby and climbed back into the front seat. Lance was beyond tired and hungry. And Marcy looked as if she hadn't eaten a decent meal in about a week.

"Another half hour and we should be at the truck stop," he told her. He took his eyes off the road for a second and glanced over to check on her.

She smiled up at him. Actually smiled. It felt as if someone had flipped on a light in a pitch-black room.

The unexpected sizzle of heat and tension made him jerk his head back around to stare through the windshield. He figured it was too dangerous to take his eyes off the road ahead. In more ways than one.

"How come you know the country around here so

well?'' she asked congenially. ''Are you from the area?''

Now, this was better. They could talk for a while. Just as long as he didn't have to look at her.

''No, ma'am,'' he said with a chuckle. ''I've spent most of my adult life following the rodeo circuit. It's a hectic way of life for a man…traveling from one rodeo town to the next. But after a few years of doing it, a guy gets to know the routes and stops pretty well. And a man can manage to make friends in the places he comes back to year after year.''

''You were in the rodeo? What'd you do there?'' Surprise colored the tone of her questions, but she sounded more awed than disgusted.

He never knew what to expect when he mentioned his work. Many people had no idea about what went on at a rodeo. Others felt it was a low-class kind of life. Still others, like the buckle bunnies and camp followers, were too easily impressed by what was really just a job.

''I was a bull rider for the first few years,'' he admitted. ''Then later I rode the broncs.''

''Cool. That's awesome. But isn't it dangerous?''

''I've had my share of bruises and broken bones, I guess. But the point is to know when to stop before it takes you down for good.''

''You don't do it anymore? You quit?''

Is that what he'd done? ''I retired from the circuit. I moved on to something better.''

''Back at your ranch in Montana?''

''The ranch isn't mine. I'm just a hired hand.''

She seemed hesitant to make a comment. ''Really?'' she finally said in a neutral tone. ''What do you do there?''

He didn't know if Marcy was truly interested, or if she'd even have the foggiest idea of what went into his job. But she was waiting for an answer. And he'd already made the decision that he wanted them to become friends.

So he figured he would just keep talking. ''The ranch was always home for a good friend of mine. His family has lived on the land for nearly a hundred years.

''They've got a formidable operation there with many different kinds of businesses. Sheep. Cattle. They breed show horses and champion stock bulls, and do lots of other profitable things, as well. My friend's dad, Buck Stanton, hired me to run the stock contracting end of the business.''

''Stock contracting?''

''Yeah. We supply the livestock to rodeos. Our operation isn't big enough yet to produce the shows themselves. But we'll be getting there someday.''

''Your ranch raises the bucking horses and those mean ol' bulls?''

The question brought an automatic grin. ''There's a bit more to it than that. I acquire bucking stock at auction, study the genetics of breeding good buckers and make sure the stock stays rank by pasturing them far away from humans.

''So far we have a crew of thirty in my division. Vets, chute men, transporters. The whole deal is growing by leaps and bounds.''

''Goodness,'' she said with a slight chuckle. ''I had

no idea so much went into that sort of thing. Have you been doing it very long?''

''Not long,'' he told her with a shake of his head.

''I see.''

There was something in the way she said the words that told him she had questions not yet spoken aloud. He just didn't know what answer to give if she wouldn't ask the question.

Nothing for him to do but keep talking. Maybe he'd hit on the right answer by accident. Plus…all this talking was helping to keep him alert and was making the time go by quicker.

''But the ranch is definitely my home now,'' he told her without a second thought. ''It's great not having to travel all the time.''

''But you're traveling now. Was this trip for business?''

His thoughts on this trip were still all jumbled in his head. Grief and regret mixed together with a final release of duty and the promise of a brand-new life. He wasn't sure he could talk about it just yet.

''No,'' he grunted. ''My grandmother passed away. I felt it was my duty to attend her funeral in New Orleans.''

''Your 'duty'?'' Marcy asked in a quiet voice. ''I don't understand.''

Hell, he'd managed to say the wrong thing after all. He really did *not* want to talk about this.

''It's not important,'' he said quickly. ''What's important is that I'm headed home. And if I'm lucky, I'll make it there by Christmas Eve.''

"Does your family celebrate that with special traditions?"

"Didn't know I had much family left. And now that Grandmother Steele is gone, I guess I'll never know much about that side of the family." Now why had he let that slip? Jeez, he was sure saying way too much to a stranger. "I hope to make the Stantons in Montana my family from now on. They've done more than give me a job—they're more like family than just friends and employers." Again, that was just too much to say. What was the matter with him?

"But you don't have a wife and kids waiting for you back in Montana?"

Ah. He had a feeling that was the question she'd been wanting to ask. He'd noted over the years that it was a question most women asked when they first met a man.

"No, ma'am. Not as yet. But I'm hopeful that'll be changing real soon. Now that I'm building a home, I intend to have everything that goes with it."

"Oh? You're engaged, then?"

He shook his head. "Not yet. But I expect that Lorna Stanton will consent to marry me when I pro pose at the family's traditional Christmas Eve party. So…no, as of this moment, I'm not engaged, either."

"Did you mean to say that this Lorna is your girl-friend?"

"I suppose you could call her a girlfriend," he admitted hesitantly. "But I've never thought of her that way. We have a lot in common. A marriage between us makes sense. It's a good solid fit."

"Hmm. So does she love you? Do you love her?"

"I can't say that we've come that far yet. But I believe the best marriages are the ones where love grows over time. I'm starting a little late in life, but we still should have fifty years or so to learn about love."

"Wait a minute." Marcy held up her hand, palm out. "You intend to ask this woman to marry you, but neither of you are in love? Have you two, uh, well, do you know for a fact that you will be compatible...in all areas?"

"If you're asking about in the bedroom, the answer is no, I don't know for sure about that part of it. But we respect each other. And that's all I'll say on the subject."

Oh, brother. Marcy could only shake her head. He couldn't be for real. She knew love was a difficult dream to realize, and this guy didn't even have the basic steps down yet.

"I kind of hate to ask this," she began tentatively. "But does Lorna know you intend to propose? Have you two talked about the possibility?"

He seemed to take a moment thinking that one over. "I wanted it to be a surprise. I thought it would be more romantic that way. Women like that kind of romance, don't they?"

Marcy bit her bottom lip to keep from laughing aloud. "Some things aren't meant to be that big a surprise, you know?"

The darkening shadows of late afternoon made the atmosphere around them suddenly seem melancholy. Marcy wished that she knew Lance a little better. He could be heading for a huge fall, and she wanted to be his friend so she could try to keep it from being such a hard landing.

He paid no attention to her attempt to warn him. ''I found a wonderful engagement ring on my last evening in New Orleans. It's an antique and very special. Wait until I tell you the crazy story of how I got it.''

They rounded a bend in the road and Lance smiled. ''The story will have to wait. You can't see it through the snowfall yet, but the truck stop is right up ahead. We'll be able to get in out of this storm in just a few minutes.''

After the waitress found a high chair for Angie, and Marcy had unbuttoned and removed the baby's snowsuit, she shrugged off her own coat and slipped into the booth beside her daughter. The place was packed and it had taken thirty minutes to get seated. Truckers, bus drivers, state police and families who'd been on their way to holiday parties, all of them had wound up stuck here waiting out the storm.

''Here's a couple of menus,'' the harried waitress told her. ''But we're not serving everything as usual. The boss wants to conserve so we can make it over the next few days without running out of food.''

''That's okay,'' Marcy said with a shrug. ''I have to check with the rest of my party, but I'd imagine we'll be having whatever you've got. And the baby will be fine if you can just bring her some milk.''

''I'll send the busboy over with a glass for her,'' the woman said. ''But it may take me a long time to get back here for your order. We're swamped. Do you mind?''

Marcy shook her head and watched the woman hurry away, disappearing into the crowds of people who were stuffed into every available table, booth and aisle. Marcy reached into her big duffel on the floor and pulled a jar of baby food, some crackers and Angie's sippy cup up onto the table.

"We'll be fine, sweetheart," she murmured to a big-eyed Angie. "It's warm here and we're safe. And I'll think of some way for us to get to Wyoming, don't you worry."

Marcy handed Angie a cracker and glanced up to find Lance making his way to their table after filling up his gas tank outside. Oh, Lord. He strode through the crowd like a man who had no trouble negotiating any obstacle. Every feminine eye in the place turned to admire his wide shoulders and the tight butt encased in slim work jeans.

With his hat in his hand and his heavy leather coat slung over one shoulder, she got her first good look at their savior. Rugged. Whoo, baby. Everything about him just screamed male.

His black hair was slicked away from his face, and he'd tied it back with some kind of rawhide string. The bronzed skin against the plaid long-sleeved shirt gave him a great outdoors appearance. A man's man for sure.

He caught her looking in his direction and focused those sharp ebony eyes on her. His wide nose bent at the bridge and looked as if it had probably been broken somewhere along the line. But it was his full lips that now captured her attention. The corners crooked up with an arrogant twist that made her throat go dry and the sweat bead between her breasts.

He eased into the booth across from her. "Nobody's been able to get a call out. The circuits are all tied up with the storm. Have you decided what you want to do from here?"

She straightened her shoulders and gulped back the nervous energy his very presence seemed to bring out in her. "I was hoping Angie and I could catch a bus to Cheyenne. Even if we're stuck here for a couple of days, a bus should get us from here to Wyoming before the first of January."

Lance shook his head. "I just talked to one of the state troopers. They're considering keeping the roads closed in both directions for the rest of the week. How important is it that you get to Cheyenne on time?"

Blinking her eyes in a short silent prayer, Marcy decided she would be perfectly honest with him. "Staying here for a couple of days and then buying bus tickets will take every dime I have. That job is my last hope, and it won't be available past the first."

He grimaced. "Unless you're exaggerating your circumstances, you'd better think of something else real quick. Because I'd say your chances of getting out of here in time have just gone from slim to none."

Three

"But...but..." Marcy was determined not to cry. This just couldn't be happening.

She took a fortifying breath and turned to check on the baby before steadying her voice and trying again. "I haven't exaggerated a thing. Angie and I will have nowhere to go if we miss this job. And I don't know what else we can do."

Lance raised one eyebrow but lowered his voice sympathetically. "What kind of job was this?"

Why not tell him? "The general manager at a hotel where I baby-sit sometimes...he's a friend really... introduced me to a rich couple from Wyoming who have two school-age kids. We all got along real well and the kids just love Angie.

"Well, the couple called my friend a few weeks ago to say they are looking to hire a nanny for their children while they all travel on a six-month tour of Europe,'' she continued. "But they intend to make a final decision on who to hire by January first so everyone can get passports and visas in time.'' The opportunity had been so perfect for her. They wouldn't mind if Angie came along.

"Traveling for six months…with children?'' Lance couldn't imagine anything worse.

Marcy looked up at him with those big brown eyes full of unshed tears, and he felt his heart sputtering in his chest. Without the scarf and old coat, she was a real stunner. Soft, blond curls framed her perfect heart-shaped face. And the dimples, button nose and long flirty lashes were terrific—but not enough to take a man's mind off her velvet voice and irresistible body.

"Yes,'' she replied. "Doesn't it sound thrilling? Just think of all the places we would see and the terrific experiences we could have. It's my dream job.''

More like a nightmare, in his opinion. Week after week turning into month after month of never settling down. Even her big, sad eyes and baby fine flaxen hair wouldn't make him consider that a dream. No, indeed. The two of them obviously had nothing in common.

While most little boys dreamed of travel and adventure, it had always been Lance's fondest wish to stay in one place—to finally have a real home where he truly belonged. His early childhood years, spent being dragged from one army base to another throughout the world, had caused him to dream not of adventures but of a big family and lots of friends in his very own stable corner of the world.

Too bad life had made other plans for him up until now.

Lance was on the verge of getting everything he'd ever dreamed of, but he couldn't stand seeing Marcy's hopeful expression. Not when he knew she was headed for a big disappointment. So he turned away from that beautiful face to look for a waitress.

"You're not likely to have the chance at that dream if the weather won't cooperate," he told Marcy without glancing over at her. "And from the looks of things, it's only getting worse outside."

"Oh, no," she said softly.

Out of the corner of his eye he saw her fussing with the baby's things. Her jerky movements made her seem like a woman who was lost and didn't know where to turn first.

Waving at a waitress passing by, Lance caught her attention and turned back around just as Marcy popped the lid off a small jar of what must be the baby's food. The baby saw what her mother was doing and reached out with one hand toward the jar.

"Okay," Marcy murmured absently to her daughter. "Don't you worry, Angie. It'll all be okay." She scooped up a spoonful of the mush and shoveled it toward the baby's open mouth.

More of the food ended up on the baby's face than went in her mouth. Marcy took a few more stabs and Lance was fascinated watching the hit-and-miss process.

The little girl had a tuft of hair on the top of her

head that was exactly the same color as her mother's. But within moments the food was all over the baby's face, dripping off her chin and sticking nastily to that little bit of hair.

He found himself smiling as Marcy sighed and tsked at her child, urging her not to put her fingers in her mouth. The whole picture tugged on some soft spot inside him.

Just then a waitress appeared with water and a glass filled with milk. "Sorry it's taken so long. This place is a madhouse. Everyone's having to pitch in and do everyone else's work in the emergency. What can I get you to eat?" She set all the glasses down on the table.

Marcy began to discuss the food possibilities with the waitress just as the answer hit him. This was the emergency that he'd been saving for. He could give Marcy enough money to get back to her family after the storm and to keep them going for a while. She must have family somewhere. That way he wouldn't have to worry about leaving her and the baby and heading off to Montana.

What a great idea, he thought with smug satisfaction. This was one way to put some of the money he'd accumulated over his years on the rodeo circuit to a good use. He would send cash back to an auto salvager in the county where they'd had to leave her broken-down car. Then even that wouldn't be a worry for her ever again. Good thing he'd thought of it.

He wanted to make her life easier. That way she might not be so disappointed when she missed her opportunity to travel the world.

"Oh, for heaven's sake. If it isn't White Eagle Steele." The waitress had turned away from Marcy and the baby and was standing with pad in hand, ready to take his order. "I'm sorry I didn't recognize you before. It's just so hectic in here. How have you been?"

Lance couldn't quite place her name. But then, he hadn't been to this part of the country for at least a year.

"I've been just fine," he said while he searched his memory for a name. "You knew I retired from competition a while back? I don't get by here much these days. I wouldn't be here now except for the storm."

The waitress laughed, and he belatedly spotted her name tag above the breast pocket of her blue-checked uniform. She wasn't one of the women he'd spent a few casual nights with, thank heaven. No, he remembered now that she'd been a fan and friend he'd conversed with on his way through this part of the world.

"Yeah, this one's a killer, all right," the waitress named Harriet said with a nod. "Looks as if no one is going to be getting home for at least a couple of days. The truck stop employees are all taking shifts… twelve hours on, then six off to grab some rest."

That gave him another idea. "Speaking of rest… Harriet. Is there a place my friend and her baby can lie down for a few hours?"

Harriet turned to look at Marcy and then at the baby. "All the men are taking turns sleeping on the driver's bunks. But there isn't much privacy for a woman, I'm afraid."

Frowning when she saw the fine lines of exhaustion
and the pale-violet smudges under Marcy's eyes, the
waitress shook her head. "Tell you what, sugar, you
eat something and then I'll find you a cot in the employee break room. Okay?"

Marcy shot Lance a quick, glaring glance, and he
was afraid she would turn down the offer. But then
she hesitantly reached over with a napkin to dab at
the baby's dirty chin and must've reconsidered their
predicament. "Okay, sure. Thanks," she told the
waitress.

That was just fine, he thought. Now Harriet would
take Marcy and the baby under her wing for the du-
ration of the storm. Things were working out just perfectly so he could leave them without feeling guilty.

Harriet finally stuffed her pad into a pocket and
told them she'd bring whatever was hot and ready to
eat. Then she turned and disappeared back through
the crowded tables.

"She called you White Eagle," Marcy mentioned
when they and the baby were alone at the table once
more. "I thought you said your name was Lance."

Had that been her focus when she'd shot him that
glaring look? "My full given name is Lance White
Eagle Steele," he admitted. "When I first took up
competition, the promoters figured it would be a novelty to have a Native American entrant. So they made
me drop my first name from the roster. Once I started
winning events they played the cowboy-and-Indian
thing up to the hilt."

Marcy nodded and almost smiled. "So, you're Native American."

Lance wasn't sure whether she was appalled by the idea or just curious. "My mother's people are Navajo," he told her plainly and without emotion. "On the other hand, my father's family, the Steeles, are as white-bread as is possible in America."

Her smile never fully formed as Marcy looked ready to ask another question. But suddenly the baby seemed to have other ideas. While her mother was preoccupied with their conversation, Angie grabbed the spoon and unceremoniously dropped it on the floor with a clatter.

"That's it," Marcy griped at her grinning daughter. "I guess you've had all the dinner you want."

Standing, Marcy unbelted Angie from the high chair. "We're going to wash up," she told him over her shoulder as she leaned over. "We'll be back before the waitress returns with the food." She pulled the baby up into her arms and took off toward the locker rooms.

Lance watched while the two made their way through the crowded tables. Damn, but the woman provided a mighty fine view from the rear. Marcy's full, rounded hips in tight-fitting jeans swayed neatly as she sauntered away.

When she finally disappeared around the corner, he was surprised to find that he'd been holding his breath until he completely lost sight of her.

This hot lusting after a beautiful woman was only normal, he assured himself. But the other warm feelings, the ones that seemed to take over his mind whenever she smiled, were downright unusual.

He wished they'd had a chance to finish their conversation. What did she think about him being from a half-and-half heritage? He'd faced every kind of prejudice over his lifetime, so it was a little startling when Marcy's response seemed more important to him than any of the others.

And he didn't know why he felt that way.

Well, he would simply have to get over it, whatever it was. By tomorrow morning he would be on his way home to Montana, and Marcy Griffin, her baby and all her attitudes would be only pleasant, and increasingly distant, memories.

Marcy dropped her spoon in the soup bowl and fought to keep her eyes open. She couldn't imagine why she felt so tired. Was the frigid weather finally getting to her?

"You look as if you can't hold your head up to eat another bite," Lance said from across the table. "Are you ready to try the cot Harriet promised?"

He was so kind. Since the moment he'd picked them up on the side of the road, he'd been the most solicitous and gentle man she'd ever been fortunate enough to meet. Now if only he would agree to take her and Angie to Cheyenne so they would be there by the first of the year. Somehow she was sure she would be able to convince him.

"You won't leave here without us, will you?" she asked him. "I mean, while we're napping you'll be sleeping, too, won't you?"

Lance scowled and for the first time she noticed how fierce he could look. Marcy had been glad to know she was right about his Native American heritage. She'd never met a real Navajo before and was thrilled to get a chance to personally know one. The idea of someone being part of the founding heritage of the country had always intrigued her.

At least, she'd thought she had been thrilled about the opportunity…until he turned that ferocious glare in her direction.

"I'll try to get a few hours in before I leave in the morning," he told her at last. "But you and the baby aren't coming with me."

His expression softened as he reached over and tenderly touched her arm. "It's better that you two go on back home when the storm is over. You'll be safer that way. I'll see to it you have enough money to keep you both going for a while."

The anger hit her fast and hard. How dare he tell her what to do? Come to think of it, the things he'd done that she'd considered as kind might be described as controlling by a more dispassionate observer.

Then again, if anyone would be familiar with controlling behavior it was her. And she felt positive that Lance had just been trying to help—in his own way.

But to think of offering her money? He really was the most arrogant…the most infuriating…the most…

She took a deep breath. He was also probably her only way out of here.

"Look," she began as reasonably as she could. "I thought you understood. Angie and I don't have a home to go back to. There is nothing for us anywhere—except in Wyoming."

"Oh, but surely your parents will take you two in until you get back on your feet." Lance dragged his hand away from her arm in order to use it to make his point. ''And that scum you—uh, your ex-husband, can certainly be made to pay child support even if he refuses to be a real father to Angie.''

Angie shrieked at the mention of her name, and Marcy dug in her bag for something she could play with. Without much thought she placed the baby's binky into her mouth and handed over the squishy, plastic dog the little girl loved so much. Angie's outburst provided the distraction she needed to rethink what she wanted to say. She had to make Lance see that he should take the two of them with him when he left.

Lordy, but Marcy hated to talk about her problems. They always sounded melodramatic when she said them out loud, and it usually seemed as if she was using them as a ploy for sympathy. But this situation was becoming desperate and it called for desperate measures.

She ground her teeth and racked her brain for a way to make him understand. ''My parents are both dead. They died in a car crash a couple of years ago. Angie and I are all alone in the world with no family.

''And as for my ex-husband, Mike...'' Marcy rolled her eyes and shook her head. ''Now that I'm legally free of him, I'd just as soon that he never has the opportunity to find Angie and me again. I can't take money from him without running the risk that he might come back into our lives.''

Lance searched her eyes and seemed to be looking for a truth that she hadn't yet made him see.

''I had a little money saved up from baby-sitting

jobs when Mike ran off,'' she said quietly. ''But it took every dime for the hospital bill and for Angie's baby doctor, and then to pay the lawyer who got me the divorce. Angie and I left our studio apartment where we'd been living right before the electric company cut off the lights.''

Yeah. It all sounded too melodramatic to her ears. But she couldn't help the awful truth. The only way she could make a difference was to change their future. And she had to make a new and better future for herself and Angie.

She just had to.

''I was at the end of the line,'' she continued. ''Trying to make enough by baby-sitting to keep food in our mouths. We were living out of that old car of mine when this fabulous job opportunity came up.''

Lance was staring with no expression on his face. She didn't know if she was getting through to him or not.

Baby Angie didn't seem to care much about her mother's story one way or the other. She spit out her binky, then squealed as she lifted her arms toward her mother. It didn't take long for her to begin bouncing in her high chair.

''Oh, Ange,'' Marcy sighed.

''What does she want?'' Lance asked. He was still trying to absorb everything Marcy had said. The two of them were really all alone in the world. Their circumstances were so far from what he'd always wanted in life that he couldn't quite get a grasp on how these two sweet females had gotten so messed up.

"Angie wants to get down," Marcy replied. "She probably needs to crawl around a little to let off some steam. But I'm just too tired to…"

"I'll watch her for you," he broke in. "While you clean up…or get your stuff repacked…or whatever. I think I can manage her for an hour or so."

Whatever had possessed him to blurt that out? He didn't know the first thing about taking care of babies.

But Marcy looked too tired to be able to care for her daughter. And he'd suddenly wanted to give her a few free moments.

"Uh, what would I have to do, exactly?" he hedged.

Marcy turned a hopeful smile to him. "Give me a second to change her and you won't have much to do." She unbuckled the baby from her high chair. "If you can find an out-of-the-way spot that's fairly clean, let her crawl around on the old army blanket. Just be sure she doesn't put anything into her mouth and that she doesn't stick her fingers into any electrical sockets, and you two should be fine."

"I won't take my eyes off her for a second. You can count on me."

Marcy stopped, stood stock-still and then turned to him with tears in her eyes. "I know we can trust you. And I can't thank you enough."

An hour later Lance was so tired he couldn't see straight. Who would've thought that a little baby could be tougher to handle than a twelve-hundred-pound bull?

He'd chased. He'd said "no, no." He'd picked her

up and put her down so many times his eyes were blurry.

And still Angie was bright-eyed and full of energy.

She lifted her arms to him once again and he smiled when he reached for her. "No wonder your mom was so exhausted," he said as she collapsed into his lap.

The baby sat up straight on his knees as he took her hands to make sure she was okay. "Hold on to my fingers, Angie. That's a girl."

She was watching him intently, and he took the minute of quiet to talk softly to the pretty little thing. "What do you see when you look at me, baby girl?" Angie didn't seem a bit frightened by what she saw. All the prejudice in the world hadn't gotten to her yet. She just looked at him with fascination and awe in her eyes.

Then she began to sway and he remembered he'd heard that babies might like to be bounced. "Horsey ride? Is that what you want?" He kept a tight grip on her while he jiggled her up and down. "Someday I'll teach you how to ride the real thing. Would you like that?"

Angie laughed and shrieked with delight. But Lance tired at last and slowed down. The baby frowned when he stopped. Then she did the most amazing thing.

She actually pulled herself up by leaning against his chest. Lance raised his hands to let her climb but kept his arms tight as she straightened her legs until she was truly standing upright.

"You actually stood up all by yourself, Angie," he said with a grin. "Just wait until we tell your mom."

He scooped her up in his arms and went off to find the baby's mother. Marcy should be ready for that cot by now, he figured. And if they were really lucky, Angie would be ready, too.

As he headed down the hall toward the employee locker room, he saw Marcy talking to one of the long-haul truckers. It was that big guy who'd been claiming he would have no trouble going West through the storm.

Lance didn't trust him any farther than he could throw him. At least, not with these two innocent females.

The decision clicked in his head as if a key had turned in its proper lock. He would be damned if they would ride with some strange trucker.

No, by heaven. They would go with him, and that's all there was to it. He wouldn't take no for an answer.

Four

"What is all this stuff? And why did you think we needed it?" Marcy couldn't help but shake her head as she glanced into the overstuffed rear compartment of Lance's SUV.

Since they'd left the truck stop behind a few hours ago, the dawn had been slowly turning the day from cold and shivery black to a slightly warmer shade of gray. She could clearly see that he'd managed to cram the back compartment from top to bottom with bags and boxes.

Last night he'd actually agreed to take her and the baby all the way to Cheyenne. Thrilled when he'd told her, she nearly hugged him with relief.

But then, as he'd stared at her with those intense ebony eyes, she'd reconsidered and thanked him profusely from a few feet away instead. Whenever they touched, and even when they weren't touching, the sizzle between them unnerved her.

"Those are supplies we might be needing if we get stuck somewhere," he told her. "I bought them at the truck stop's convenience store. Fresh water, blankets, snacks. It never hurts to be prepared." He watched the slick road ahead and didn't turn as he spoke.

"Oh? Were you a Boy Scout?" Marcy sank back into the passenger seat and nearly groaned in pleasure. This SUV was luxury all the way. Compared to her old rattletrap, Lance's transportation seemed like a limo.

"Nope. As a child I was never in one place long enough to get the opportunity. But I spent my teen years on the rez learning the responsibilities and duties required of an adult male member of the Dine." He kept on staring straight out through the windshield. "Most of that stuck with me."

"The 'Dine'?"

"That's the name the people of the Navajo Nation use when they refer to themselves."

Lance fell silent, and she glanced into the back seat to check on Angie. The rumble of the SUV's big engine had lulled the baby to sleep.

Marcy ran her hand over the smooth surface of the tan leather seats and sighed. The snow had stopped falling hours ago and this back road they were traveling had been plowed quite recently. Everything would be fine.

She wondered if Lance would like some conversation for a while. He was probably rather tired from only managing a short nap last night, and perhaps he needed companionship to help him remain alert. She wanted to do her part.

"You said you didn't stay in one place as a child," she began tentatively. "I've always wanted to see the world. Travel. Can you tell me about where you lived while you were growing up?"

A few long seconds of silence had her wondering if he wouldn't rather that she keep her mouth shut and leave him alone to concentrate on his driving. But then he cleared his throat and began to speak in hushed tones. She guessed it was an attempt to keep from waking Angie.

"My father is a naval officer. Before I was born he graduated from Annapolis...and all the very special things that go along with that." The sarcasm in his voice let her know what he thought of the occupation she'd always greatly admired. "After I was born, he was stationed in ten countries in eight years. My mother and I didn't go to all of them, but we did follow him to most of the places. Italy, Japan, Korea, Hawaii, the Philippines. It's all a blur now."

"They sound great," she told him. "I was raised in a backwater town in southern Illinois. I dreamed of seeing all those wonderful places. Of going anywhere, actually."

He shook his head slowly and slanted her a glance out of the corner of his eye. "It was no dream for me. I always longed for a place to settle. For a big home that I would know so well it would become almost boring. And for a chance to get to know other kids long enough to be able to call them friends."

"Sorry," she squeaked in as small a voice as she

could manage. "I hadn't thought about it that way. What happened after you turned eight?"

"My mother died."

Oh, man. Talk about stepping out of one mess and going right into a pile of dog do-do with the next step. When would she learn to keep her mouth shut?

"After we buried Mother, my father took me to his mother's home in New Orleans and dropped me there so he could proceed on with his career," Lance continued. "And before you ask, no, I didn't get to be at home with my grandmother either. She had never been terribly thrilled with her son's choice for a wife and was appalled by my lack of schooling and knowledge of the social graces. I was barely alone with her for a couple of weeks before she sent me off to a series of boarding schools."

Hmm. Didn't sound like the loving grandmother that Marcy had always wished she'd had. This poor guy hadn't had much of a family life at all.

She should've known better than to open her big mouth. But no…

She twisted under her seat belt to face him. "Then how did you get to a reservation from the boarding schools?" The question had been asked with a naive stupidity she would soon regret.

He blew out a breath, but went right into his explanation. "It took my mother's people a long time to hear of her death. She had only distant relatives left living on the Navajo reservation in northeast Arizona. When they learned she was gone and that my father had abandoned me to his mother, they made an appeal to the tribal authorities to have me returned to my ancestors' homeland for instruction in the way of the clan.

"Seems they had both tribal and federal law on their side," he continued with a sour look on his face. "It took them a few years, but at the age of thirteen I was sent to live in Arizona and learn the way of the Dine."

"My goodness. You were sent there? It sounds like you went to a prison."

The corners of his mouth curled up, and Marcy wasn't sure whether the movement was meant as a snarl or a smile. She wished back the words but knew it was too late.

"It was no worse than the boarding schools had been," he confessed. "At least I knew they wanted me."

"Oh. Well, that's good, right?"

Lance rolled his shoulders and she could see the tension in his muscles. "It was good that I learned Navajo culture. About how the land and the family are important and must be protected. I'm glad I know now about the ceremonies—and the Navajo view of life.

"And I never would've become an expert horseman if I hadn't gone there," he went on. "Those lessons gave me the rodeo, and believe me, that was one of the best things that ever happened to me."

The words ripped out of him, making Marcy think that what he hadn't said was more important. He hadn't said that he'd found the home he'd been yearning for, and she suddenly realized he'd said absolutely nothing about friendship or love.

In a flash of insight, she realized that he had never belonged anywhere. Not in his father's world of travel, books and manners. And not in his mother's world of land, ancient culture and ceremony.

Her heart ached for him, but she didn't know how to let him know what she felt. Marcy was sure it hadn't been sympathy he had wanted when he told her all this. Hoping with all her might that what he'd really wanted from her was friendship, she sat back in her seat and closed her eyes. She'd finally figured out that there were times when it would be best to just keep her mouth shut.

Lance fiddled with the radio, but all he was getting was static. That pretty much summed up the bulk of his life so far.

He slid a glance over his shoulder to check on Angie. Her woolly hat had slipped down over one eye as she snoozed peacefully in her car seat. His heart thumped at the sight of the precious little darlin'.

He'd recently come to the conclusion that children were a big part of what he wanted out of marriage and making a home. He wanted his own baby girl who would look up at him in awe the same way that Angie had done last night.

The powerful ache of wanting a home and family of his own suddenly became so overwhelming that he was forced to find something else to think about. He turned his head to check on Angie's mother, who'd fallen asleep in the front passenger seat.

But the pain of wanting most certainly did not dim

with a look in that direction. It just changed in intensity.

She looked all soft and warm…and sexy as hell. Her fine, blond hair was tousled and curled around her face. Her mouth was in a smug, sleepy little pout, with the rosy bottom lip puffed out. The picture she made was of a beautiful sleeping woman who'd been recently and thoroughly loved.

A flash of the same desire he'd felt when he'd told her that he'd take her and the baby to Cheyenne tugged at his gut and sent his mind spiraling down the wrong path. The expression on her face last night as he'd said his piece had quickly gone from hopeful to grateful, and finally settled into need. She'd wanted him as much as he'd wanted her. He was just sure they felt the same draw.

Almost. He'd almost leaned in for the kiss that would've been heaven—and totally inappropriate for the circumstances. He'd raised his hand to touch her face. Her eyes had widened and became the color of rich hot chocolate. He'd almost felt how soft her skin would be against his fingers if he drew them down the satin of her jawline. Almost.

But when the baby had fussed in his arms and someone had jostled against him in the truck stop hallway on their way to the locker room, he'd come out of the sensual haze with a jolt. That had not been the right place for such a move. And she was most definitely the wrong woman.

Well, not exactly the wrong woman. In fact, he believed she would've been perfectly right for what he'd had in mind. But she wasn't Lorna. She wasn't the woman he'd decided he would be happy spending his life with.

Certainly he could keep his hands to himself and his brain from heading south long enough to get back home and ask Lorna to marry him. Couldn't he?

He rubbed at his chin and looked around the interior of the vehicle, realizing at once that the SUV had grown too warm and the inside of the windshield had fogged over. Someone must've been doing some heavy breathing.

He was starting to lose it. He needed to think.

Stretching his back muscles and surreptitiously rearranging his too-tight jeans in one smooth move, Lance tried to remember the responsibility lessons he'd learned from the Dine.

The Four Directions. That's it. He would review the Four Directions of life in his mind.

East was the direction of dawn. It would be as good a place to start as any since it was just past dawn now. And East was the thinking direction. Thinking was something he'd better start doing real soon.

Let's see…how did the lesson go? A Navajo should think first before he takes a step. Consider each move carefully.

Yes, that was what he had done when he'd decided to marry Lorna. He'd made the decision that they had a lot in common and would be good mates. He was rather proud of himself for coming to such a sensible conclusion.

Marcy moaned softly in her sleep and restlessly changed her position under the seat belt. The sight and sound of her all of a sudden sent his brain back down under his own belt. Shoot. There went thinking for the time being.

With his mind off in places where it shouldn't be, Lance didn't see the gaping pothole in the road until it was too late to keep from hitting it with the right front tire. The vehicle dipped violently and a thunking sound rattled noisily through the SUV. Hell.

Marcy stirred and opened her eyes. "What…?"

The baby in the back seat came awake in a flash of fury and fright. In seconds her screams built to nerve-racking.

"It was just a pothole," Lance told Marcy over the din.

"You'd better stop so I can check on Angie and try to calm her down."

It would probably be smart for him to stop and check the tire, anyway. He pulled off the road as far as he dared without getting stuck in a snowdrift. They were traveling on a lonely stretch, alongside some rancher's desolate range land. He'd already noted the barbwire fencing and had been watching the fierce, high-plains wind pile swirling snow deeply up against every post.

He left the SUV running, with the heated exhaust streaming backward in a frosty haze, but he remembered to pull on the parking brake. Expecting Marcy to climb over the console and between the seats like she did the last time, Lance ignored her, hunched down in his coat and stepped around the hood to check on his front tire.

The tire looked fine. He kicked it once for good measure, then reached down to run his gloved hand along the tread. These were the extra heavy-duty radials and he was fairly sure they should hold up to a few bumps and jolts.

Behind him, he heard a door open and shut. By the time he turned to see what was going on, Marcy was out of the SUV and fighting the wind, trying to pull open the rear compartment door.

He stepped behind the vehicle and stood between her and the blasting bark of frigid air. "What do you need in there?" he asked, yelling over the wind gusts toward the back of her head. "I thought you could reach what you wanted from the back seat."

Lifting the tailgate above him, Lance loomed over her body as he tried to block the worst of the wind. He stepped closer and was surprised to feel her warmth clear through both their layers of clothing. Even with the wind roaring at his back and in her direction, he was close enough to catch a whiff of sunshine and talcum.

It was Marcy's special scent, he knew it immediately. Her hair just looked like it would smell of sunshine, and the other scent had to be somehow baby-related. Nice, he thought. Homey.

But his body was reacting to the smell in an entirely different manner than his mind. Nice and homey, hell. Horny was more like it. He gritted his teeth and stepped back as far as he dared without having the wind whip through the SUV and possibly knocking Marcy to the asphalt.

She bent to dig through the mass of boxes and duffel bags stacked in the back. "You shoved all these new sacks in on top of the old. I can't find the baby's bag.''

Kneeling on the edge of the cargo compartment and nearly climbing right inside, Marcy kept on searching. ''I think I found it,'' she finally hollered over her shoulder. ''At least I've worked the bag's straps free. It's buried.''

All he could see from this vantage point was a curvy, rounded female bottom, covered over in skin-tight jeans. ''Let me get it for you,'' he proposed. ''The wind's too cold for you to be out here this long.'' And he was afraid he couldn't stand watching her much longer without touching.

''I've got it,'' she grunted. ''I just need to give it a good tug.''

He bent his head, trying to see what she was doing. Using both hands and her entire upper body, Marcy was in a tug-of-war with two half-buried plastic straps held down by a huge mound of heavy luggage.

''Here. Let me help…'' He inched forward to grab the straps at the exact moment they snapped.

She yelped and came flying backward. Fortunately, his body was right there to catch her, but the momentum threw him off balance and he slipped on a patch of ice. Both of them landed on the road, with him lying flat on his back and her on top of him and grinding her rounded fanny tightly against his crotch.

Uh-oh. Now she was bound to feel the truth of what she did to him.

Using every bit of the agility he'd honed on the rodeo circuit and a hell of a lot more determination than he was feeling at the moment, Lance twisted his

body and dragged them both to their feet in one
smooth move. When they were righted, he discovered
that one of his hands was holding her arm at a point
way too close to her breast and his other hand was
firmly splayed against her stomach.

It was tough letting go.

Cursing silently, he dragged his arms to his sides.
There was no chance he would be able to look her in
the eyes right now, so he glanced over her shoulder
to where the baby still sat, crying in the back seat.

"Sorry," he managed on a ragged breath. "Now
get in. And I'll bring you the damn bag."

She couldn't seem to find a comfortable spot and
tried squirming under her seat belt. The move earned
her a silent glare from the driver.

They hadn't said a word to each other since the
embarrassing incident with the bag that had taken
place several hours ago. Feeling a flaming-red rash of
shame creep up her neck again, she thought back to
how preoccupied she'd been while trying to do her
best for Angie. Angie needed a change, and the diapers were in her bag. And Marcy had also wanted to
find the packets of restaurant crackers she'd secreted
into the bag, hoping to give them to the baby and
take her mind off the loud noises of the potholed road
and the howling wind.

But then those darn cheap straps had broken, sail-
ing her backward right on top of Lance. At first the
surprise took her breath away. But as she'd hissed in
a lungful of the crisp air, it had dawned on her exactly

what she had landed on—and the realization left her gasping and breathless all over again.

Amazing. Just sitting in the same car with him was making them both all hot and bothered. But she'd thought…she'd imagined…that he had been immune to the electricity. He seemed so stoic and…oh, what was the word? Well, she couldn't think of one that really fit, but *unemotional* was as good a description as any.

And here she'd found out with one shocking swoop that, even out in the savage, freezing wind, he had been thinking of her in the same way she'd been dreaming of him. She could barely get her brain around the idea. This unusual need. This wild and crazy craving to have him touch her, to touch him in return, was a shared sensation.

All this time she'd known he was intense, but she'd never noticed the hunger in his eyes before. Hadn't he told her he intended to marry a woman he'd never slept with yet? Such an idea seemed exactly the opposite of the lustful look she'd seen in those black-as-night eyes.

A sudden sharp turn in her thoughts had her crossing her arms over her chest and sitting up straight in her seat. Could it be possible he was the same kind of no-good character she'd run into often during the past nine months who figured a divorcée was fair game? Good enough to take to bed, but not suitable to take home to the family?

Well, if that was his game, he could just stay in his silence-filled bubble for the rest of the trip for all she cared. As much as she had liked the novelty of talking to a real adult, Marcy was no stranger to silence.

In fact, she had grown to love the quiet of the reference stacks in her hometown library so much that she'd spent much of her childhood there. Reading, dreaming of faraway places and the exotic people who would live there.

Going away in books had been a pleasure. And a refuge from her parents' arguments at home.

When her ex-husband, Mike, had first come to town, he'd been so charming and talkative. Of course, she'd never felt the tingle of tension down her spine with him that Lance had been creating in her over the past day. But Mike had talked and talked. Mostly of taking her to see the big wide world, and of all the places he'd been and all the places where her soul had longed to go.

They hadn't known each other a full month when she married him and left her boring life behind.

Ha. That was such a joke. They had ended up traveling a grand total of several hundred miles to a cramped apartment in Minneapolis. And there began a new boring life of tiring menial jobs, no money and no pleasure. Sneaking away from it for a few hours to sit in the warm, quiet treasure of the public library, once again had helped her hold onto her sanity.

No, indeed. Silence was no enemy of hers. For much of her life it had been her only friend and companion.

"Are you getting hungry?" The sound of his voice broke through to her and she turned to stare at his profile.

"Hungry? Me? Not really."

"Well, I am. We've been making pretty good time since the snow stopped falling late last night. But we're going to have to stop for gas soon." He didn't turn his head to look at her, and she wondered if he was still embarrassed.

"Will we make it to Cheyenne before Christmas?"

"I'm still hopeful I can get you there and be at the ranch before the Christmas Eve party is over."

"Oh. Well, that would be great." So... Lusting after her had apparently not changed his mind about asking someone else to marry him.

Marcy was afraid his motives were a lot more complicated than what she'd first imagined. She shook her head softly to herself and vowed to remain aloof.

Friends...lovers... Rats. She didn't have the time to be anything with Lance White Eagle Steele. And it was a darn good thing she'd realized it before the fantasies carried her away.

"We're about to enter an area of western South Dakota called 'the Badlands,'" he told her. "I spent a lot of time around here during my rodeo days. In fact, I know a place right up the way where we can fill up the SUV and have a good meal all at the same time."

He glanced over to her with a crooked smile on his lips. "Just relax and think of warming your body in a friendly atmosphere and of tempting your mouth with a delicious home-baked dessert. That'll make you hungry."

Oh, yeah, she thought as she closed her eyes. Just the deep, smooth sound of his voice was making her hungrier than she'd ever been in her whole life. Darn it.

Five

Marcy sat on a stool at the counter and stared up into the violet eyes of one of the most stunning women she'd ever seen. Thick, rich, mink-colored hair framed that face the same way the long, dark lashes framed those fantastic eyes.

"Marianne, this is Marcy and the baby's name is Angie." Lance stood right behind her stool, holding Angie in his arms and talking to the gorgeous woman behind the counter as if they were dear old friends. Or maybe something more.

"Welcome, Marcy and Angie. I sure hope you're hungry." Marianne wore a sweater of deepest amethyst that matched her eyes, and her smile was as wide and genuine as her words.

Marcy folded her hands in her lap, stared down and absently worried about the loose threads in her old gray coat. "It's nice to meet you," she murmured without looking up. "But Angie only needs a few crackers and a glass of milk. And I'll be just fine with coffee. Thanks." She couldn't help but compare her own worn, dull clothes to Marianne's beautiful outfit, and ended up wishing she could find a quiet hole to crawl into.

She finally glanced up just as a look passed between Lance and Marianne. Yep. There was definitely a history between these two.

"I'll go find a high chair for Angie," Marianne said. "You folks sit at a table and make yourselves at home."

Lance handed the baby over to Marcy. "I'll help."

Marianne shot a glance in Marcy's direction. "No need. I'll be right back."

There weren't many patrons in the small café, but then, it was midafternoon and the day before Christmas Eve. They removed their outerwear and arranged themselves at a quiet table in the corner and, before Marcy knew what had happened, she was digging into a big plate of homemade chicken and dumplings. Angie had her own plate with chopped up pieces of the same meal, and Lance was helping to spoon them into the baby's mouth.

The place was warm and homey, just as he'd said. Spotless and decorated in a western theme, the café looked prosperous. And that darn, tall and gorgeous Marianne had been more than kind.

Marianne came out of the kitchen and stood beside their table. "If everything's okay here so far, I'll bring the deep-dish apple crisp as soon as it comes out of the oven. I think you'll love it.''

Marcy tried to say no thanks, but her mouth was too full to protest that she couldn't possibly eat dessert on top of everything else.

Lance smiled at their hostess and ducked his head as Angie tried to feed him a fistful of her dumplings. ''That'd be great, thanks,'' he said to Marianne. ''By the way, how's Hank doing? Where is he today?''

Marianne rolled her eyes toward the ceiling. ''On the roof. He's shoveling off the snow accumulation before the next storm hits later.''

''I'd like to see him while I'm here. Maybe I should go lend him a hand.''

''After you finish dinner you can go up on my roof and work it off if you feel you must,'' Marianne said with a wry smile. ''Go out the back way when you're done. I know he'd love to see you, too.''

Marianne went into the kitchen and Marcy choked down her last bite. ''Here.'' She took the spoon from Lance's hand. ''Let me clean up Angie while you finish eating.'' She set aside Angie's plate and dug into the bag for one of the wipes that Lance had bought at the convenience store.

''Marianne is a nice lady,'' she said casually as Lance polished off his dinner. ''Have you known each other long?''

''About ten years, more or less,'' he replied between spoonfuls.

''Were you two, uh…''

Lance slid his empty plate across to a vacant spot and leaned his elbows on the table. ''If you're asking if we were a couple, the answer is yeah. Once. A long time ago."

There went that big mouth of hers getting her in trouble again. But he was studying her with such an intense perusal that she'd lost her mind. Those black onyx eyes looked over at her from under thick, dark lashes, and Marcy could swear lightning bolts zinged out of them.

Well, if she'd already been rude, she might as well go all the way. "What happened?"

He shrugged a shoulder. "Timing wasn't right, I guess. Mostly she wanted to settle down, and I wasn't done being a bronc rider yet."

"But now you are settled down. You have a home."

"So does she." He waved a hand around at the interior of the lovely café. "Marianne has been happily married for over four years to one of the best rodeo clowns I ever knew.

"Hank once was one of the finest athletes on the circuit…until he shattered his leg one too many times. Now he runs a terrific restaurant and busy filling station. He's from this part of the country…with deep roots and family."

Marcy shook her head. "But that seems so sad. That you and Marianne didn't want the same thing at the same time."

Lance sat back in his chair and crossed his ankles in front of him. "Things work out the way they're supposed to. Sometimes, no matter how much you think you want something, it just isn't going to happen.'' He took a breath. ''And that's usually for the best.''

Boy, did she ever know about that. She was beyond grateful that Mike had dumped her when he found out about the baby. The only good thing he'd ever done for her was Angie. And his leaving gave them an opportunity for a better life.

''When I was a kid, I thought if you lived right and were good enough, that you'd meet the right person, fall in love and be happy ever after,'' she said quietly. ''I thought it was like magic. But it isn't, is it?''

''Magic?'' One corner of his mouth turned up in a half smile, half scowl. ''No. I don't believe in magic. I believe that everyone makes their own choices and opportunities.''

Yeah, she believed in people taking charge of their own destinies and figured he must believe that, too. Otherwise, why would he be preparing to ask a woman he didn't love to marry him?

She let her gaze slide over the black T-shirt and jeans he wore beneath his heavy coat and nearly fainted when she saw his bulging muscles flex and stretch under the material. What woman in her right mind would say no to him?

But the story of his and Marianne's failed romance was all simply too sad to contemplate. And soon he might be heading for the exact same kind of failure.

Marcy wished with everything in her that she could turn back time and believe in the magic once again.

Lance stood next to their empty table with his hands folded behind his back and stared out the floor-to-ceiling window at the snowy scene beyond the café. He should've been thinking of the ranch and of how his wranglers would be getting on with their various jobs, though he knew they would do just fine. But all he could see in his head were babies.

He'd started out by thinking about Angie and of how she would manage, traveling the world with her mother—of how she would look as she grew into a beautiful child. It didn't take long for that image to evolve into pictures of other babies. Babies with dark eyes and hair that looked just like his.

Absently he rubbed at a spot over his heart and blinked his eyes. It would happen for him soon. He would make it happen.

"She's lovely." Marianne spoke softly from behind him and interrupted his thoughts.

"Huh? Who?" Lance turned away from the wide picture window and faced her in the now empty café.

"Marcy. She's lovely. I showed her where she could change the baby and freshen up," Marianne told him. "This is the first woman you've brought here. I can see that she's special to you."

He shook his head a little more vehemently than he'd meant and took a step back. "It's not like that. I rescued them from the side of the road and I've promised to take them to Cheyenne. I hardly know her."

Marianne tilted her head and pursed her lips. "That brings up another good question. Just what are you doing so far from home in the dead of winter? You haven't bothered to come for a visit since you moved out to that ranch in western Montana. Why come now, so close to Christmas and in one of the worst blizzards we've seen in years?''

He felt the perverse grin sneaking out around the corners of his mouth. ''Impatience. Stupidity. Arrogance. Take your pick.'' Easing the bus pan from her hands, he started gathering dirty dishes off the table. ''I got it in my head that I had to be back at the ranch by Christmas Eve. And neither the worst blizzard in memory nor all the flights at O'Hare being cancelled was going to stop me.''

''Christmas Eve? That's tomorrow night and you have to stop first in Cheyenne?'' Marianne looked confused. ''What happens if you don't make it there on time?''

''Then what I planned to do on Christmas Eve will wait for a few days.'' He slid the last of the plates and silverware into the gray plastic pan. ''Looking back on it now, I'm not too sure why I thought it was so important to be there on a certain date. But I just did.''

Marianne swiped a wet cloth over the table and chairs and straightened up with a quick glance out the window. ''The weather's changing. That last front must be coming through. It's ten degrees warmer than this morning and the wind's died down some.'' She turned her chin to look at him but nodded toward the window. ''It's already starting to snow again. If you want to help Hank, you'd better scoot.''

He hefted the bus pan into the kitchen while Marianne trailed behind. ''I won't be long,'' he said. ''Tell Marcy where I've gone and have her wait inside till I'm done.'' Dropping the pan on a counter, he turned to head out the back door.

Marianne stopped him with a gentle hand on his arm. ''Whether you want to admit it or not, she *is* special to you. You look at her like you want to gobble her whole.''

Stopping midstride, he swung around and sputtered out denials.

She just smiled. ''Deny it all you want. But there was a time when I would've given a year of my life if you'd ever looked at me that way. In your heart, she *is* different.''

He took a deep breath and ran a hand across his mouth before he spoke. ''My heart has nothing to do with anything. We don't want the same things. And after I drop her and the baby off in Cheyenne, we'll never see each other again.''

Marianne watched him in silence, still smiling softly.

''I swear, we haven't so much as touched,'' he protested. ''And I don't *intend* to ever touch her, either.'' It burned a hole right through his gut to say that— and mean it. But there were some things you just didn't do. ''We've only recently met and she's going to a new job. A job that will take her overseas for six months.''

He shook his own head now, trying to clear it. ''I'm in the middle of building a home in Montana on the ranch. It's the first place I've ever felt that I really belonged.'' He set his jaw and turned back to the door. ''Whatever might've been between us is impossible.''

Before he could put his hand on the doorknob, Marianne had one more thing to say. "Impossible or not, Lance. You can't just turn your back. Not if what you will be missing is a chance at magic."

Speechless and suddenly angry, Lance muttered under his breath. Another fanciful female and that "magic" junk.

Hell.

He slammed out the door and drew in a deep lungful of frosty air. Everything he'd ever wanted was waiting for him back at the ranch in Montana. Another few days and all of this would be nothing more than a fading memory.

At least…he could only hope so.

Marcy shifted the baby in her arms and walked into the café's kitchen. "You have a lovely home, Marianne. It's so convenient to your restaurant. Thanks for letting me use it to clean up and change Angie."

"You're most welcome. Have a seat." She dried her hands on a cloth towel and nodded at the kitchen table. "Lance said for you to wait for him here where it's warm. He's outside irritating my husband while he finishes up on the roof." Marianne chuckled, tossed the towel and pulled out two chairs so they could sit down.

"In the spring, Hank and I are planning on enlarging the café," Marianne told her as she arranged the baby so they could sit together. "And by next fall I'm hoping we'll be able to add on to the house. It depends on how the business does."

"How do you like living so far out in the country?'' Marcy propped the baby on her lap. "Lance told me that your husband has roots and family nearby. So I suppose he's happy here. But how do you like it? Are you ever lonely?''

Marianne's smile broadened into a grin. "Heavens no. Lonely? That's a hoot. We're so busy with the business that I barely have time to take a bath, let alone think about being lonely.''

Angie started to fuss. Without asking, Marianne reached around, picked up a clean spoon and handed it to the baby. "Besides, it was me that wanted to move back here and start this business.

"Hank has a brother, Bobby, who lives west of here about fifty miles. Bobby and Lance were competitors and best buddies on the circuit when Bobby fell in love with a friend of mine. At about that same time, Bobby was offered a job at the new casino that was opening up on the reservation in Pine Ridge and he decided to move back home and settle down.''

Marcy jiggled Angie as the baby tapped her spoon on the wood table.

Marianne patted the baby's cheek and smiled. "Bobby has two kids and a terrific house on ten acres now. He's doing great and they're real happy. After Hank and I started going out, we would stop in to visit with Bobby and Vicki when we'd get a moment free from the circuit. I began to yearn for a simpler life with no traveling and a big family all around me.''

"Were you with the rodeo?'' Marcy realized too late the question might be another blunder, but...

Marianne just laughed. "I did barrel riding as a

teenager. But I wasn't the best. After a few years I took charge of one of the concession stands... hamburgers, tacos and nachos...you know?''

Marcy nodded and breathed a little easier. She'd heard of women who did nothing but follow the rodeo around the country so they could shack up with the cowpokes along the way. She was glad to know that Marianne wasn't one of that kind.

"Anyway, after Hank's last big tumble," Marianne continued, "the one that put him in the hospital for six months...I decided it was time for us to do something different with our lives." She waved a hand around at the industrial-looking kitchen and the stainless equipment. "I've always been a good cook, so this was a natural."

"Your food is wonderful," Marcy told her. "I'm glad your business is doing well." The baby picked that moment to pitch the spoon on the floor, so Marcy began to rock her softly.

"Thanks," Marianne said with another one of those dazzling smiles and picked up spoon. "Does Angie need anything else?"

"No. She's getting sleepy. If I rock her a minute, she'll probably nod off."

Marianne stood up. "Then how about her mother? Can I get you anything? A cup of coffee, maybe."

"No, thanks. I'm still stuffed." She sat back in her chair and let Angie relax against her chest. "Are you going to shut the restaurant down for Christmas so you can be with your family?"

"Yes, it's the one day of the year when we won't open at all." Marianne quietly poured herself a cup of coffee and returned to the table. "But the whole family won't be able to be here. Bobby and Vicki and the kids have gone to Florida to be with her parents for the holidays. Hank has other brothers and his parents live nearby, but we'll miss Bobby and Vicki."

Marianne sipped in silence for a few minutes, watching Angie as her eyes drifted closed. "He really is a very special man," she whispered at last.

"Who? Your husband, or his brother?"

"No," she chuckled. "I mean…yes, of course Hank is wonderful and I love him very much. But I was talking about Lance being the one that's so special."

"Oh." Marcy wasn't sure she wanted to hear that from one of his old lovers. But this time she decided not to say anything.

"He tells me that you two just met," Marianne began again. "I thought you might like to know what kind of a person he really is."

Yes…or…no. Shoot, Marcy couldn't decide what she wanted when it came to Lance. She did want to get to know him…maybe even become his friend. But they only had a day or so left together. Maybe it would be better if they stayed strangers.

She remained in indecisive silence for so long that Marianne seemed to accept that as a go-ahead to keep on talking. "It would take me all day to tell you everything he's ever done that was extraordinary. So I'll just say that he would give his right arm to help a friend in need. I've seen him do seemingly impossible things when someone he cared about was in trouble."

Marianne set her cup down and sighed. "As a personal example, he lent Hank and me the money to start this business." She looked around at her gleaming appliances. "None of the banks would consider lending money to a couple like us with no experience and huge hospital bills to pay. But we didn't even have to ask Lance. He heard of our trouble and simply handed us a check. When the first year nearly put us out of business, he came through with another loan then, too."

Marianne stood and took her cup to the sink. "Now, I'm not saying that the man is a saint, mind you. In fact, there was a time when I would've gladly wrung his neck." She turned her back to Marcy and the baby, rinsed out the cup and cleared her throat. "But shortly after that I found out that he'd lent Bobby the money to build his ranch house. Lance even pitched in on his days off and helped Bobby put it together with his own sweat."

She'd been speaking over her shoulder but now she dried her hands again and returned to the table. "We've paid Lance back every cent we owed him, and Bobby has, too…as soon as he started work and could get a mortgage. But that's not the point.

"The point is that Lance would give a friend his very last penny if that friend was in need—and never think about it twice." Marianne laid a soft hand on Marcy's shoulder. "He's a good man. The best. And I wanted you to know how the rest of the world sees him."

Marcy had been aware that Lance was a different sort, better than any other man she'd ever known. Marianne's words only confirmed her own thoughts.

But she didn't have the slightest idea what to do with her newfound knowledge. Deathly afraid that she was beginning to fall for him, Marcy wondered if she could manage to hold on to her heart for the small amount of time they had left.

Everything she'd dreamed about waited in Cheyenne. Now all she had to do was keep Lance out of her dreams long enough to get there.

When Lance finally bundled Marcy and the baby into the SUV, the snow was coming down at an impossible rate. The temperature hovered right below freezing, bringing the snow to the ground in wet and heavy clumps.

It was dark and still, the sun had set hours ago. And the blinding snow was going to make driving slow and tedious. He shouldn't have spent so much time with Hank. But what else was he supposed to do when he realized how tough it was for the man to steady himself on the roof with his bum leg?

Lance was glad he'd helped him out. Hank and Marianne were good people. Hadn't she insisted that Marcy take a couple of thick pairs of socks and one of her extraheavy parkas? All right, so maybe the coat was a few inches too big and absolutely bright red, which made it seem much more suitable for Marianne's coloring than for Marcy's. But it would certainly keep Marcy warmer than that old, threadbare coat she'd been wearing. It was a very nice gesture for Marianne to make.

For the next hour he inched the SUV along down the plowed highway. He prayed that the wipers would hold up to the snow and keep the windshield clear enough for him to see the road ahead. Thirty miles later he knew it was time to stop and shovel the snow off by hand. It was thick enough now to make convenience-store slushies.

"Why are you stopping?" Marcy asked with a yawn.

"I need to clear the snow." He stepped out of the SUV, but only stayed outside for long enough to swipe his arm across the expanse of glass. Before he was seated back inside, the snow was thick again.

"Should we turn back?" The tension and fear in Marcy's voice made him wish they had never started. He didn't want her to be afraid. He would take care of them. It was only a snowstorm.

He shook his head and set the transmission in low gear. "We've come too far. If we keep going, we may outrun the worst of the storm. It seems to be passing over our heads at a pretty good clip."

Actually, those words sounded hollow to his ears. Like wishful thinking. The truth was, with every mile they traveled, the snowfall worsened. But turning around would be crazy. Best to keep moving forward.

Down the road in another half hour, a different problem presented itself. The highway they were on had obviously been plowed earlier today, but now it was drifting over under buckets of snow flurries.

Before he had a chance to wonder if they should keep going under the onslaught, he caught sight of deep tire tracks in the road ahead. Looked as if a semi was moving along the same highway just in front of them. He breathed a little easier and kept his eyes trained on those tracks.

Flicking a glance in Marcy's direction, he saw that she'd gripped the door handle and her knuckles were white with tension. She hadn't seen the tracks of their fellow traveler yet and her whole body was tight. He needed to take that panic off her shoulders somehow.

Clearing his throat, he started talking in as calm a voice as he could manage. "Looks like we're right behind a trucker. If he thinks the road is good enough to navigate, then I'm not too worried. We'll follow his tracks."

She didn't make a comment and he figured he'd better keep on talking. "Do you need to check on Angie? She's been awfully quiet."

Marcy released a pent-up breath, and he was glad to know she was at least breathing. "The baby's asleep. It's dark and warm and cozy in here...for her."

Marcy's voice wasn't all that steady. But he'd gotten her to talk and breathe. That was something.

"I sure wish it was daylight so you could see the scenery," he quickly told her. "The mountains and rocks in the Badlands are spectacular. Giant, craggy peaks tower over the road right in this section. They make a phenomenal picture. Just like a postcard."

As soon as the words were out of his mouth, Lance saw red taillights flashing directly up ahead. He gingerly put his foot on the brake, hoping he had enough time to come to a stop without skidding off the road.

Marcy hissed in a breath. "What's going on?"

When the SUV slowed to a halt, Lance put it in

Park and pulled the Stetson lower on his forehead. "I don't know but I intend to find out in a minute."

As soon as he'd walked ten feet, he immediately saw the problem. But it took him fifteen minutes to discuss potential solutions with the handful of truckers that had gathered out in the storm and stood gabbing in the middle of the road.

By the time he climbed back in the driver's seat, he'd come to a decision. "The road's closed," he told Marcy. "The heavy snow caused a slide. It'll take hours, maybe a day, to dig it out."

"What are we going to do?"

"Half a mile back we passed a side road that leads to a friend's house," he said in a fairly steady voice. "It's no more than three miles off this road to his ranch. We'll go there. Wait out the storm until they clear the road."

"A friend? What friend?"

He took the SUV out of Park and eased it into a 180-degree turn. "Hank's brother, Bobby, and his wife, Vicki. You'll like them."

"No."

The sudden panic in her voice caused him to put on the brakes so he could turn and really look at her. "What…?"

"We can't go there," she said with a nearly hysterical crack in her voice. "Marianne told me Bobby and his wife are in Florida for the holidays. They aren't at their ranch."

She put her hand on his arm and squeezed. "What are we going to do?"

Six

"**D**on't panic." His voice was smooth and low, and a smile touched the corners of his mouth. "We can still find shelter at Bobby's ranch. I helped him build the place, and I know where they keep everything. Bobby and Vicki won't mind if we stay there until the roads are clear."

It wasn't so much Lance's words as his calm manner that gave her the hope everything would be all right. "Well, if you're sure they won't mind." Marcy pried her fingers off his arm and tried a hesitant smile. "I'm a little concerned about Angie."

The minute she'd said it, she realized it was not the baby who was frightened. In fact, Angie seemed to be holding up quite well to this harrowing trip. Marcy had seen plenty of snow while growing up back at home, but this storm and the thought of being lost in a blinding blizzard was driving her to distraction.

It was also true that baby Angie hadn't needed to worry about fighting off *both* the elements and a nutty desire for the man who was seeing them through. Every minute, every mile brought Marcy closer to falling for the guy. She couldn't listen to his baritone voice without having a spark of need combust low in her belly. He couldn't so much as touch her arm without igniting a blaze that made her nearly blind with wanting to have him touch her everywhere.

It was crazy. It was erotic. She was toast.

Lance started up the SUV again and made sure the four-wheel-drive system was operational. "There's no need for Angie to be frightened. This is more of a snowsquall than a real storm." He shot her a wicked wink, and Marcy felt a shivery tingle begin in the base of her spine.

"The farm road off the highway that leads to Bobby's ranch may not have been plowed," Lance advised. "But we'll take it nice and slow…so Angie won't be scared."

Marcy ducked her head and looked through the top of the windshield at more tons of falling snow than she'd ever before seen in one place at one time. Some "squall." They'd be lucky if they weren't buried in it before they reached the ranch.

Lance drove on in the silent darkness for about twenty minutes. She watched as he tried to follow the fence posts along the side of the road. But he seemed to recognize different landmarks as they went, and Marcy felt the tension begin to leave her shoulders.

"The gate to Bobby's ranch road isn't easy to find at the best of times," he muttered. "But it should be right up the way."

"Is the house very much farther after we turn?"

"Not far. Maybe a quarter of a mile."

His answer set her teeth on edge, and she hunched her shoulders again. What if Bobby's road was already buried in six feet of snow? What would they do?

Just as she was picturing the worst possible scenario, Lance said with a huff, "There it is."

But as he turned the steering wheel, she felt the SUV slide on the icy buildup. Lance smoothly twisted the wheel in the same direction as the slide the way he should've, but the SUV did not respond. In a whirling flash of flying snow and the loud crunching of tires on ice, the back end of the SUV swung wild.

Before she could let out the scream that was building, the left rear of the SUV sank into a deep hole and ground to a halt. Suddenly they were immobile and tipping precariously to the port side. Marcy held her breath, waiting for something worse to happen.

Lance sat and studied their position for a few moments. Then he turned off the key. "I suspect that's as far as we're going tonight. Give me a minute to check how badly the rear end is buried."

She didn't want to be left alone with the baby. "No, wait. I'll go out with you. Together maybe we can push the SUV out of the drift."

Lance stilled, turned to face her and touched her shoulder with his gloved hand. "Trust me, Marcy. I won't be more than five feet away from the SUV the

whole time. If I find there's anything we can do together to free us, I'll let you know.

"Stay with Angie," he admonished. "If she wakes
up, you need to be where she can see you. I'll only
be outside for a few minutes...tops."

Marcy inhaled deeply and nodded her head. She
did trust him and needed to get her fears back under
control.

He unbuckled his belt and shoved open the driver's
door. The SUV listed to that side, but he managed to
get the door open far enough to escape into the
blowing storm.

After he closed the door behind him, she unbuckled
her own belt and twisted in her seat to check on the
baby. So far, Angie hadn't budged. It would probably
take a little time for her child to notice the lack of
motion, become aware of the growing chill and wake
up.

Marcy wondered how long it would take for the
interior of the SUV to cool, now that the motor and
the heater had been shut down. She was afraid it
could get really frigid in here...really fast.

Before she had the opportunity to become too concerned about their situation, Lance jerked open the
back right passenger door. A blast of cold air crashed
into the interior of the SUV, and Marcy found herself
up on her knees and pushing through between the
seats to reach Angie in that same instant. All she
could think of was reaching her suddenly awake and
sobbing child.

"The tire landed in a snowdrift that was covering
a ditch," Lance hollered over the noise of wind rush-

ing through the SUV and the baby's cries. "It would take some time before we could free the tire. But it's still snowing and I don't want to take any chances with you two. We'll be better off hiking to the ranch house. I'll come back and retrieve our things after I make sure you're safe."

She didn't like the idea of hiking with Angie in this weather. But there didn't seem to be much choice. And in the meantime, Lance was working to release the baby from her restraints.

He pulled Angie free and captured her against his chest with one strong arm. Then he bent over the seat and with his free hand dragged out the army blanket from the rear compartment.

"Button up your parka," he demanded. "The temperature is dropping again."

Marcy flipped up the hood on her parka and scrambled out of the back seat. Dropping into snow that was deep enough to reach clear up to her butt, she had to grab Lance's arm in order to steady herself. How were they supposed to walk in this mess?

After catching her balance she stood beside Lance, trying to ignore being half buried in snow while she tightened up Angie's snowsuit. Pulling the baby's cap down tight, she realized Angie had stopped crying the very moment that Lance picked her up. Now her child's eyes were growing wide as she began to pick up on her mother's fear. Marcy cautioned herself to calm down.

Lance took a quick inventory of everyone's clothing, checking the snaps on all the coats. "I don't want you walking in those lightweight shoes," he told

Marcy with one last tug to make sure everything was buttoned down tightly.

He handed Angie over to her, then put the blanket over both their heads. "You carry the baby. I'll carry you."

"What…?"

Without another word, he swept her off her feet— baby, army blanket and all.

"But, Lance… We're too much for you. I can walk."

"Of course you can walk," he said with a smile in his voice. "But the snow is three feet deep already. And if we don't get to the ranch shortly, it may drift over the road another foot or so. You can't walk in snow up to your chin."

Marcy tightened her arms around Angie and closed her eyes. She felt safe and warm next to his chest and began to relax.

In a few more moments she leaned her cheek comfortably against his shoulder. She could hear his heart, beating in strong, even pulses as he strode effortlessly through the building blizzard.

Marcy lost track of time but soon noticed Lance's breathing become labored. Her first reaction was embarrassing. All of a sudden she wanted to hear his breath catch that same way while they were making love. She could picture him, laboring above her to give them both the ultimate pleasure.

It was an exciting thought. And it drove an electric jolt straight through her.

But then the reality of their current, dire situation

flashed in her mind. What had gone so wrong that he suddenly needed to work hard? It also seemed their walk had taken too long. Had he become blinded by the swirling snow? She'd read of such things happening, and the thought of it produced nightmare images in her head.

"We've arrived," Lance announced right at that moment. "I'll just carry you up onto the front porch before I set you down. It's covered and fairly dry. Then I'll go retrieve the keys and let you two inside."

She felt him climbing what must have been the stairs. When he gently lowered her to her feet, she peeked out from the blanket.

"Stay here," he thundered. "I'll be back in a few minutes."

As he disappeared, Marcy tightened her grip around the baby. Angie had fallen fast asleep against her shoulder and now lay there like a heavy lump of mashed potatoes.

Marcy checked their surroundings. They were standing before a wide door, underneath an overhanging cover that dipped low toward the ground on the front side. A light next to the door illuminated the porch, or it might have been as dark as a cave. Bobby and Vicki must have their outside lights on a timer.

Without the warmth of Lance's chest, the cold began to seep right into her veins. She stomped her feet in an effort to stave off the icy sensations creeping steadily inside her clothes and beginning to numb the lower half of her body.

Moving closer to the door in a fight to get out of the wind and stay a little warmer, she hoped that

Lance would hurry back. And she tried to bury the fear that coming here was a big mistake.

Meanwhile, Lance was fighting with the combination lock on the storage building attached to the side of the house. The temperature had all of a sudden dropped dangerously low, and his fingers refused to work properly. He knew the cold meant that the snowfall would probably slow soon. But then in short order the wind would drive what was on the ground into huge drifts covering everything over with a blinding haze of white.

He needed to pick up the keys and get back to Marcy and the baby fast.

At last the lock clicked open, and Lance didn't waste a second reaching inside for the house keys that he knew were hanging on a nail just inside the door. Once he had them, he jammed the lock shut and headed back to the front porch.

When he first rounded the corner of the house, he didn't see the two females. Oh, man. Marcy hadn't stepped out into this whirl of snow, had she? He set his jaw and prepared for the worst.

"Marcy," he called over the roar of the wind. "Where are you?"

When he heard a muffled noise coming from a darkened alcove on the porch, his heart started up again. Closing the distance between them in two hefty strides, he wrapped his arms around both of them and began moving toward the front door. The key went smoothly into the lock and the door thankfully swung open with little trouble.

"Let's get you two inside and warm," he said with a gruff voice.

After shuttling them inside and slamming the outer door behind him, Lance flipped on a light and moved the whole group forward into the great room. "You stand in here a second, but don't take off your coats until I have a chance to turn up the thermostat."

He unwrapped the blanket from around their heads and let it drop to the floor. Most of the accumulation of snow had already dropped off it onto the porch. As Marcy's face came into view, his breath caught in his chest. The tip of her nose was pink, which he hoped was actually a good sign. But her eyes were glazed and her cheeks were the palest color of white he'd ever seen on a human.

Not sure what to do for her first, he felt conflicted. But he had to do something—and fast.

"Don't try to move," he croaked. "Wait."

Lance never moved so fast in his life. In seconds he had pushed up the heat. He blessed Bobby for leaving not only the heat on, and set at about fifty degrees, but also for leaving logs placed in the raised hearth. Even the kindling was already set out under the grate.

He opened the flue and lit a match, watching while the fire caught before closing the glass fire door in front of the hearth. That should warm things up in here within a few minutes.

Turning back to Marcy, he saw she was shivering so violently that Angie was beginning to stir against her shoulder. He took the baby from her arms.

Vicki had left a thick afghan slung across the back

of the sofa. He wrapped Angie up in it tightly, and then laid her on the cozy suede cushions.

Returning to Marcy, he wasn't sure what the best thing to do for her might be. Her teeth were chattering as she swayed uneasily on her feet.

He didn't take the time to think. Swinging Marcy up in his arms, he hugged her close and stepped nearer the hearth.

"It's all right," he murmured, more to himself than for her benefit. "You'll warm up in a minute. Everything will be fine."

He closed his eyes and prayed that he was right. She just had to be okay.

The fire raged behind the glass doors as he stood there quietly praying. He couldn't remember ever having been so afraid.

Nothing much had so affected him in the past. Not the rodeo with bulls charging and stomping faster than he could get out of their way. Not even the bucking horses on the ranch that might mean the end of a career with one wrong twist. No weather, physical pain or even long periods of being alone on the road had put this kind of gut-wrenching fear in his belly.

The more he thought about it, the more he realized only one time in his life had he come close to this kind of horrific panic. And that was when his father had dropped him off at his grandmother's house at the age of eight—leaving him lonely and scared beyond imagining.

But this time the gnawing fear seemed much worse. Marcy. He suddenly realized that she'd come to mean more to him than he'd thought. A tiny drop of sweat beaded at his temple and ran down his neck.

She shifted slightly in his arms, and he leaned his cheek against her forehead. "You feeling the warmth yet?" he whispered into her hair.

"It's better," she murmured. Her shivering had all but stopped, and her voice barely shook at all.

He felt the tension leave his shoulders, and his heart returned to its normal rhythm. She was truly going to be all right.

The relief was so profound that he automatically pressed a kiss against her forehead. The skin there was soft and warm next to his lips and he lost himself in the sensual sensations. Before he knew what hit him, he wanted to taste of her. To breathe in her scent and let his hands move to whatever part of her body they pleased—to wherever they might please her the most.

"You can put me down now," Marcy said quietly. "I need to check on Angie."

Right. She was right. He had to quit dreaming about things that would never happen, and let her go.

Carefully he eased her to her feet and then held on while she steadied herself. "Are you really okay? Do you need to thaw your hands and feet under some water?"

"I can't feel my feet yet." She pulled out of his hands and moved to Angie who was sound asleep. "But that might be a good thing."

Marcy knelt down next to the sofa and gingerly unwrapped the afghan he'd cuddled around her child. The baby's eyes stayed closed. But as her mother continued unbuttoning the heavy snowsuit, Angie crinkled up her face and began to cry.

"Oh, good," Marcy breathed with a sigh. "She probably needs a change and she might be hungry. That means she's okay."

"I know Vicki packed away some old things in the attic that belonged to her kids," he told Marcy. "I helped store them but I don't remember exactly what she saved. Maybe some diapers. Their youngest is almost four now, so it's been a while."

Marcy kept her back to him as she removed the baby's shoes and mittens and rubbed at the tiny feet and hands to get the circulation moving. "I can make a diaper out of a kitchen towel as a temporary fix," she said over her shoulder. "But if there's a baby bottle, it would be wonderful. I'd like to get some warm water down her as soon as possible." Marcy shrugged out of her parka and let it pool around her knees on the floor.

"I think you both could stand to sit in a warm bathtub until you get the feeling back in your fingers and toes." He took Marcy's shoulders and pulled her to her feet. "Come on. I'll start the tub and put a kettle on the stove for hot water. Then I'll check out the attic."

She picked up the baby and let him lead them to the guest bathroom. He'd built this section of the house himself and had deliberately designed it to his specifications. After all, he was the guest that had visited most often, and the bed and the bath needed to be his size.

He showed Marcy where the towels were kept.

Then he checked to be sure the water heater was working and that the water had not frozen in the pipes. When the water came cascading out of the spigot, he once again blessed Bobby for remembering all the things he'd taught him. In the dead of winter, it paid not to skimp on fuel and cause more problems than money saved.

Leaving Marcy and the baby in the bathroom, Lance lit the stove and put a pot of water on to boil. Then he headed for the attic.

Vicki had marked the boxes, and it was easy to find the bottles and baby-size dishes. In a quick survey, he could see there were no boxes marked Diapers. But a baby's crib, in several pieces, leaned against a back wall. He hauled up the dish and bottle box and decided to come back for the crib later.

In ten minutes he'd washed out the baby bottles, made some tea for Marcy and set aside a bottle with hot water for Angie. He hoped Marcy liked herbal tea. Women seemed to like the stuff, and he'd heard that it helped to settle your insides when things were tense.

He felt a little tense himself at the moment, but he didn't particularly think that a cup of tea would help.

While taking the tea and the bottle into the guest room, Lance made a quick decision about what he should do after he delivered them. He knocked on the bathroom door. ''I've got some hot tea and a baby bottle full of hot water out here.''

He listened but didn't hear a sound. ''You okay in there, Marcy?''

"Yes," she called through the door. "Can you bring them in? My hands are full."

Him, in there? With her in the bathtub? No way.

"How about if I set them just inside the door?" he asked like the chicken he was.

He opened the door, set the cup and bottle down on the other side and backed out without ever lifting his eyes from the floorboards. "Here you go. Check the temperature on the bottle before you give it to the baby. Okay?"

"Yes, thank you, Lance."

"Uh." He wasn't sure he liked talking to her through the closed door, but it seemed to be the only way at the moment. "I've decided to go out to the SUV and pick up as much of our stuff as I can carry. I'll bring the baby bag for sure. You two will be all right without me, won't you?"

"Are you crazy?" Her voice rose an octave. "Please don't go back outside. It's dangerous."

Had anyone else ever worried about his welfare? He couldn't remember if they had. And it warmed him to know she cared that much. But he couldn't stand here smiling at the back of a closed door when they needed his help so badly.

"It'll be fine, Marcy. Don't worry. I think the blizzard is just about over. I'll be back before you know I've been gone."

Before you know I've been gone. Jeez. She'd felt his absence the moment he'd left the house.

And nearly an hour later she was flustered, way beyond scared, and heading right for hysteria. The

conflict of wanting to go out and find him warred with
the knowledge that she couldn't leave her child alone.

The bath had warmed both her and the baby. After
drying off, she'd put their dry clothes back on. Then
she'd rummaged through Vicki's kitchen, hoping to
be forgiven for the emergency, and found some
canned milk. Angie had taken the milk and fallen
sound asleep in her arms. Marcy snuggled her on the
wide sofa in front of the fire again and set pillows
around the baby so she wouldn't roll off.

But now Marcy paced the floor in the foyer, fisting
her hands and listening intently for any noise that
might mean Lance was returning. Had he been snow-
blinded and lost his way?

He was such a good man. It was perfectly clear to
her that somewhere along the line he'd given up his
own desire to be home by Christmas Eve in order to
take them to Cheyenne. She was sure they wouldn't
even be leaving this house until long after Christmas
Eve was over. The thought that he could be so selfless
had tears stinging in the back of her eyes.

She shook her head, wanting to find some anger in
order to see her through. Mad. She should be downright furious that he'd taken a chance with his life just
so they could have a few meaningless things from the
SUV.

But she couldn't muster even a thread of mad toward him. The only thing in her mind and in her heart
right now was need. Need to see him. To touch him.
To hold him to her heart where he would be safe and
warm.

Marcy stormed over to the sofa and checked the

baby. Lightly touching her child's forehead, she sniffed and murmured a soft lullaby. "Don't worry, baby," she crooned. "We *will* make it to our bright future. All of us will make it, I promise."

The front door suddenly creaked open behind her. And Marcy held her breath as she spun around to be sure it was Lance. He closed the door and stomped his feet, then set his bundles down. Finally he flipped off the Stetson and slapped it against his jeans.

He was really safe. Her heart started to beat again in double time. Thank heaven, he was safe.

She squeaked with relief because she couldn't find her voice—couldn't even manage to breathe until she touched him and assured herself that he was really here and this wasn't just a dream.

Covering the distance between them in a run, she threw herself against his chest. In one quick move she jumped, wrapped her legs around his waist and plastered his face with breathless kisses.

For half a second Lance seemed startled. But in the next moment he hugged her close to his body, found her lips with his own and pressed a searing kiss against them. It was all heat and desperation. Shocking and erotically passionate.

He nudged her lips apart with his tongue and filled her mouth with the taste and feel of him. Blinding desire skipped across her nerves, leaving her stunned and tense.

Lance took tiny nips at her lips with his teeth, then soothed, laving them with his tongue. She couldn't think. Could only feel and react.

She heard a moan and realized it had come from

deep inside her own body as he rained kisses down on her face and neck. The sound rumbled through her veins like a train in a tunnel, bringing fire and arousal to the surface. In flames, she only wished to brand him with the same fire that had ignited within her.

Those lips of his that had rushed over her skin with need and little purpose suddenly slowed and began to linger. He gently brought their mouths together, touched her lips, then retreated before bringing them together again for a soft, plundering caress. It slowed the action but pumped up her need.

Driving her fingers through his hair, she tried to devour him in one bite. She didn't want slow and sensual. She didn't want him to think—to remember he was about to ask someone else to marry him.

Marcy wanted that quick flash of desire. The relief that the fusion of two bodies could bring.

Nothing else.

Seven

With his heart thundering madly against his ribs, it took every ounce of strength Lance had left to break off their kiss. Since the first time they'd touched, the blood boiled in his veins with every glance in her direction. And having her in his arms now with her legs wrapped around his waist was causing his iron control to falter, pushing him beyond needy.

His body hardened, and what was left of his mind turned to mush, as he imagined what it would be like to bury himself deep inside all that warmth. But he had never taken advantage of a vulnerable woman before. And considering Marcy's desperate need for him to keep her and the baby safe until they reached Cheyenne, at the moment she just might be the most vulnerable woman he'd ever known.

So, kissing her this way and giving in to the urgent demands of his body was a really bad idea.

Hell. Hell. *Hell.*

He relaxed his arms and let her slide slowly down until her feet rested on the floor. "I need to take this coat off, Marcy. I'm getting you all wet and cold again." He set his jaw, took hold of her shoulders and held her away. "And I'm dripping all over the floor."

Heavy-lidded eyes lifted to his, and the same need he felt burning in his gut shone brightly behind her confused stare. "What?"

"I brought in the diapers, and a change of clothes for both of us," he said. What he'd wanted to say was, "Please let me hold you and keep you warm through the storm." But he didn't...couldn't.

"When it's daylight, I'll go back out for the rest of our things. But it's late now and I need a shower," he managed instead. "Let's get settled and try to sleep for a few hours. By tomorrow morning we can see where we stand with this storm."

"All...right." Her face was flushed, and she blinked a couple of times.

This just might turn out to be the toughest thing he'd ever done. "Let me get changed and then I'll bring the crib down from the attic for Angie."

She frowned for a second but soon her eyes cleared and she smiled up at him. "A crib? How wonderful." Glancing over her shoulder at the baby asleep on the sofa, she said, "I think Angie will appreciate the diapers, too. I used a towel after her bath, but it can't be very comfortable."

No, and his jeans weren't at all comfortable at the moment, either. Tight and confining, they reminded him that he needed to take control of his needs.

Hell.

He bent and handed her the diaper bag. "You two enjoy yourselves. I'll be back in a few minutes."

Brushing past her with as much dignity as he could muster, he made a hasty retreat for the attic. With one swift curse under his breath he stomped up the stairs, swearing to keep a minimum of ten feet between them for the rest of their time together.

Well before dawn Lance gave up on the idea of getting any sleep. Every time he shut his eyes, memories of the soft, moist velvet of Marcy's lips came back to devil him.

He'd been too distracted to rest. Achy, needy and burning with unwanted visions, he'd tossed and turned but could find no comfort or peace in the blackness of night. He had nowhere to hide from the erotic images of Marcy's body clinging to his.

Normally, he could sleep anywhere. On the circuit, he'd been known to sleep on a blanket in the back of his truck. He even remembered snoozing on the floor of a horse trailer one night when he didn't want to leave a sick horse alone.

This time, though, even the comfortable suede cushions on Bobby and Vicki's sofa couldn't soothe the electric tingle running just under his skin. And Marcy was at fault for all this. He just couldn't get her out of his head.

Last night after that spectacular kiss, he'd set up

the crib for Angie in the guest room and settled in Marcy and baby for the night as quickly as he could. He hadn't liked what having her in his arms had done to him, and he frantically strove to keep her at arm's length.

This morning he'd rolled off the couch and almost crawled to the bathroom on his hands and knees. First he splashed his face with cold water, but that didn't slow down the unwanted thoughts. So he dove into his second frigid shower in less than six hours and stood there long enough to make his toes numb.

But nothing seemed to help.

Hell.

He started a pot of coffee brewing, then dug around in the pantry looking for something to fix for breakfast. Keeping busy should help alleviate this misery. Shouldn't it?

Marcy was really special. Beautiful, a great mother and easy to talk to, she was all a woman should be and much more. But that wasn't entirely what he needed in his life. He wanted…no…he *demanded* a woman who would be happy settling down on the ranch.

For most of his life he'd put aside thoughts of building a place to call home. Family and home hadn't mattered in the scheme of his life. Or at least he'd kidded himself that they didn't matter.

But the more money he made and the more he traveled, the more he realized that something huge was missing from his life. When Bobby and Vicki built this house, and then Marianne and Hank married and settled into a steady life, Lance had realized that it was a home base that he most wanted. A place where there were special people who cared. People who thought he mattered.

He'd never before known such a place.

About that same time Buck Stanton had taken him under his wing and offered him friendship, a job and a place to call home. Lance had jumped at the chance. He was more than ready to build that friendship and that place into something important.

And as wonderful as Marcy was, she didn't want to settle down. To her a home was a place of confinement—a prison. Something to escape while she traveled the world and sought out adventure.

No matter how much he wanted to take comfort from her, Marcy and her sexy lips were simply not on his agenda.

Digging out a box of pancake mix and a bottle of maple syrup, Lance turned his thoughts to eating and decided that pancakes would be as good a breakfast as any on a cold morning. Needing something to take his mind off Marcy's sensual body, he poured the mix and water into a bowl and began beating the hell out of it. He managed to force away any thoughts of taking her to his bed by daydreaming about the ranch and having his very own family there someday.

Still half-asleep, Marcy pulled Angie from her crib and rocked the fussing baby in her arms. "Shush, Angie. It's too early to get up."

Angie was having none of that. Marcy laid her daughter back into the crib and changed her diapers, hoping that might settle her down. It had been a really long night. One of the longest.

Marcy couldn't imagine what suddenly changed inside Lance last night. But she knew the sizzle that had passed between them was real and full of electric impulses. He had definitely been interested. *More* than interested, she was willing to wager.

Her stomach did a sudden back flip when she thought about how his black eyes burned when he'd let her slide down his body. Oh, and that hard body of his was something else she would never manage to get out of her mind, either.

But he *had* let her go. Forced her to go, really. And the first thing out of his mouth was about a crib for Angie.

Maybe he could only think of her as a mother to her child. Marcy knew he liked her well enough and was positive she'd felt his desire. But maybe he couldn't get past the idea of her being a mother. Some men were like that, she knew.

In fact, her ex-husband had said that women lost their sensuality when they became mothers. To him it had been the ultimate turnoff.

Angie was dressed and dry, yet still she whined.

"Come on, baby," Marcy whispered as she swung her up and settled her against a shoulder. "Let's go fix you another bottle of that canned milk. You must be hungry."

Marcy tiptoed down the darkened hall, trying not to wake Lance. He'd insisted that she and Angie take the guest room last night, saying the sofa was ex-

tremely comfortable and that he could sleep anywhere.

She'd had her doubts about the comfort of that
sofa. It was big and wide and the cushions were soft,
but still it wasn't like the queen-size bed in the guest
room. That bed had been the ultimate in comfort. And
comfort was something Marcy had nearly forgotten
while she and the baby had been out of their little
apartment over the past month.

As Marcy turned the corner to enter the kitchen,
she saw a light and heard a rustling noise. Then she
saw him. His back was to her as he stood cooking
something on the stove.

Her breath hitched. Lance was so beautiful. He
didn't have a shirt on, and the muscles across his wide
shoulders were bunching as he worked. Those arms
were sinewy and bulging with power, and watching
them did something to her insides. Something erotic
and far beyond her experience.

His long black hair swung free and hung below the
bronzed skin of his shoulder blades. Sleek, his hair
was wet, all shiny and satiny soft.

He bent slightly to reach something, drawing her
attention to his narrow waist and down farther to his
tight butt encased in slim jeans. Her mouth watered,
but it had nothing to do with the good smells coming
from whatever he was cooking.

Fussing against her shoulder, Angie couldn't see
the spectacular sight that had captured her mother's
total attention. The baby squirmed in Marcy's arms,
and her whining finally culminated in a yelp of urgent
hunger pains.

Lance turned toward them at the sound. His dark, rugged gaze made him seem every bit as hungry as Angie. Only, not for food.

Whew. That look could thaw any woman's frozen senses. And Marcy's senses were anything but frozen at the moment.

Suddenly it was too hot in this kitchen.

He raked his gaze from her sock-clad feet to her I-forgot-to-comb-it hair. Marcy did a quick inventory. She'd slept in her sweats and socks and hadn't bothered to so much as brush her teeth or hair before she'd stumbled down the hallway.

Well, shoot. This picture wasn't going to do much to change his mind about her not being sexy.

She watched while he swallowed hard and cleared his throat. "Good morning," he said with a rasp. "It's a little early, but would you like breakfast? Put Angie in the high chair. I'll have pancakes ready in a minute."

"Uh. I just came to fix Angie a bottle."

The expression in his eyes went lukewarm, and she felt as if she'd somehow disappointed him. "But the pancakes and coffee smell wonderful," she quickly added. "Just give me a few minutes to feed Angie and I'd love to have breakfast with you."

The food was wonderful, and Lance turned out to be a surprisingly good cook. But she'd barely tasted anything while she'd been trying hard not to stare at his naked chest across the table.

At last she stood to move their dishes to the sink.

"Leave them," he told her in a low voice. "You take care of the baby and I'll see to the dishes."

The sound of his voice ran erratically over her nerve endings. She set the dishes in the sink, turned on the water and shoved a hand through her unruly morning hair. With her back to him she grimaced. It was all she could do not to run to the bathroom to clean up so she would be more presentable.

"That's okay," she gulped. "You're really good with Angie. Why don't you watch her for a few minutes while I do the dishes?"

"Will it be okay if I put her on the floor?" he asked hesitantly. "We built this place to be baby friendly, but I don't want to do anything you might not approve of."

His concern warmed her but didn't do much to stop the tingles that moved toward her belly when he spoke in that dripped-honey voice. "Wipe her face with a wet cloth first," she managed. "Then you can put her down."

She shot a glance over her shoulder and saw him tenderly swiping the cloth across Angie's mouth. A sharp twist in her stomach reminded her that she'd never seen a man be so gentle. Oh, what she would have given for Angie to have that kind of father all along.

The surprise longing for someone to care about her and Angie hit hard. Suddenly a dish slipped out of her hands and clattered against the counter. "Sorry."

"It didn't break. Don't worry," Lance said while he took Angie from the high chair. "Did I tell you that Angie actually stood up all by herself the other night? Maybe I can coax her into doing it again so you can see.''

''Uh…'' It took all of Marcy's willpower to quickly dry their dishes and stack them. ''Fine. You two work on that for a while. I'll go change and be back in a few minutes.''

Dashing out of the kitchen, Marcy gulped in deep breaths. Everything was so messed up.

She desperately needed to reclaim her resolve to find a better life for herself and Angie. Wanting a man, no matter how spectacular he might be, had never before taken precedence over the rest of her life.

Okay, so this man was tender, caring and had a good heart. And the sight of his bare chest did things to her insides that her body barely recognized. So what?

Marcy had already taken a huge risk with her life when she'd married a man who tried to control her every thought and didn't love her enough to stay and accept their child. How could she even be considering having sex with this man when he was ready to marry a woman he didn't really love?

Shaking her head with chagrin and trying to rid herself of the leftover sexual tension, she stripped and stepped into the shower. A splash of cold water did nothing to soothe her unsettled body or harden her melting heart.

A few hours later she waited for Lance to return to the house from another trip out to the SUV. Marcy was determined to find ways to keep her mind occupied.

It was Christmas Eve and the poor guy was just about to miss his party at the Montana ranch altogether. He'd told her earlier that, though the snow had stopped, it didn't look as if they'd be able to dig the SUV out of the ditch until tomorrow.

She'd spent some time searching through the kitchen cabinets and had found popcorn and hot chocolate mix. Maybe she could make him feel a little better about missing the family party back at his ranch by putting together a cozy little Christmas Eve for the three of them. It seemed like the least she could do.

He was taking a long time outside again, and it was jangling her nerves. She went to a window and quickly discovered that the view had been blocked by windblown snow. No wonder it had seemed too dark in here for midday.

Marcy checked the rest of the windows and found they had all been buried by snow buildup. A tiny shiver of claustrophobia left her hunching her shoulders and taking deep breaths.

Digging into the refrigerator and pantry with a vengeance, she decided to make a Christmas Eve celebration that would be just what they both needed to take their minds off their current situation.

By the time Lance came stomping into the mud room, located off the kitchen, loaded down with bags and duffels, she had slice-and-bake chocolate chip cookies in the oven and all the materials gathered for stringing together popcorn and defrosted cranberries. It was something she remembered her mother had done while they waited for her father to come home from the local bar on Christmas Eve. Many Christmases he never made it home at all.

"Mmm. It smells good in here," Lance said as he shrugged out of his coat and entered the kitchen.

Looking up just in time to catch a glimpse of broad shoulders and a scrumptious butt in tight jeans as he bent to check the oven, she completely lost her train of thought. Darn, but he was the sexiest man she had ever laid eyes on.

"I'm baking cookies, and I thought later we'd have hot chocolate," she murmured with a quiet sigh.

"That sounds nice. What are you doing now?"

She held up the popcorn bowl. "I'm going to string popcorn and cranberries. After that, I'll try to make a few decorations with flour. Maybe it'll be at least a little festive in here. I hope Vicki doesn't mind that I've used her things."

"She won't. In fact, I know she would be more than happy for you to use anything you find. She's one of the most generous and giving people I know." He settled his large body into a chair at the kitchen table next to her. "Can I help?"

The question took her back a second. "Really?" She had never known a man who cared about anything as sentimental as Christmas decorations.

He nodded. "Please? But you'll have to show me what to do."

"Sure." She handed him a length of string and a fat needle and demonstrated the proper technique.

Lance fumbled with the cranberries, but under Marcy's gentle tutoring he started to get the hang of it. Part of his trouble was that he couldn't concentrate with her bending over him and guiding his hands with her own. She giggled when he stuck the needle in his finger, and the sound of her laughter undid him totally.

When he'd first stepped inside and caught a whiff of the homey smells of popcorn and cookies baking, his knees went weak with pleasure. This was just as he'd always pictured how a home should be.

He couldn't wait until the day when he would come in from the cold to find his own baby in her crib taking a nap, good smells coming from his own oven and his loving wife waiting at the kitchen table. As he tried to shirk off the familiar desire for a home, stronger, more urgent needs began to seep under his resolve and assail his senses.

Whenever Marcy moved closer, he caught a whiff of a scent much more sensual than cookies. He recognized that sexy sunshine smell, along with the unique smell that belonged to Marcy alone. It stirred his body in ways that he'd promised himself he wouldn't go.

With a shake of a shoulder, he decided that what they needed right now was to talk. Listening to her laugh, and sitting here soaking up the clash of those smells, was dragging his senses into overdrive and could not be a very smart thing to do.

"Do you always have a big celebration at Christmas?" he asked her.

Her expression went still for a second, then she smiled sadly. "I've never had what you might call a 'big' celebration. My parents couldn't afford to do a lot for Christmas. My mom always tried to compensate by making me little gifts. But in my opinion the best part was that she was off work and could spend time with me.''

She looked so serious that he was sorry he'd ever brought it up. He needed to find something else to talk about to take her mind off her past Christmases.

Shifting uncomfortably in his seat, he felt the rough edges of the ring box he still carried. ''I never finished telling you the story of how I came to have the antique ring, did I?'' As he came to the end of a string of popcorn, he handed it over and began again. ''It was really such an odd thing. At a late hour, I came barreling out of the funeral parlor in New Orleans where my grandmother's service had just been held.''

In his mind, he could see the dark scene and feel the pain of a loss he didn't know how to explain. ''I wasn't thinking too clearly. I guess I was all wrapped up in wanting a relationship with my grandmother that would never happen.''

He looked into Marcy's eyes and felt an immediate bond. But that was also something he couldn't have explained if his life depended on it. So he let himself wander back to that night in New Orleans.

''Maybe I walked in circles, I don't remember. I only remember that suddenly a home and a family to call my own became the most important things in the whole world. I lost several hours while I stumbled around wishing I had someone to go home to.''

Marcy reached out and placed her hand over his. But the touch only confused and confounded him. He jerked back and stood.

"How about I make us that hot chocolate while I finish my story?" he asked as he stepped away from the table. "I think I can manage to do two things at one time."

He couldn't remember why it had seemed so important to tell her this story. But all of a sudden it was imperative that he finish. And it was hard to think when she was near.

"Anyway," he continued while he picked up the instant hot chocolate packets and tore them open. "I began to daydream about Montana...of how I'd felt at home there for the first time in my life. Then I thought of the people on the ranch and how much I wanted them to be my real family."

He sighed and stood with the packets suspended in his hand as he lost himself in the memory of that night in New Orleans. "It came to me in a flash. If Lorna and I married, I would really become part of her family. The whole problem suddenly had a simple solution.

"My life would have a purpose. In my head I could visualize the steps that were necessary to make my dream happen. I tried to go through the Navajo's Four Directions, the things that would take me to my goal. First to the East...the thinking direction. But I figured I had thought about it enough...all my life it seemed. So the next direction was South...to plan."

A strangled chuckle escaped his lips as he remembered how he had planned to buy a ring, fly home for Christmas Eve and begin his new life by asking for Lorna's hand in marriage. It had sounded so easy.

His voice grew rough, but he had to tell the story.

"It was late by then, and even in the French Quarter most of the retail stores were closed. But I was determined not to fly home without an engagement ring. My plan called for a ring. I wasn't going to ask her without one."

"Lance…"

Marcy's voice captured his attention, but he put his palm out in a gesture to stop her from getting up. "No, let me just tell you what happened," he urged. "I was headed toward a shop that I thought might be open when I rounded a corner and bumped into an old gypsy woman.

"It was the strangest thing. I knocked into her pretty hard and when she staggered, I stopped to make sure she was all right. She was ancient-looking and so thin I was afraid I had really injured her. But before I could ask how she was, she called me by name."

The memory still shook him. "Really," he mumbled as if to assure himself it was true. "She said, 'Have no fear, Lance White Eagle Steele, all is as it should be.'

"I was taken aback by her words, let me tell you. And I was just about to ask her if she recognized me from my rodeo days when she reached into a pocket in her dress and pulled out a ring box. 'I have something for you,' she said and shoved the box into my hands."

He looked down at the hot chocolate packets in his hand, but it was the box he was seeing…remembering. "It was like I was suddenly in a trance. I opened the box and there was an antique engagement ring. It stunned me, it was so close to what I had envisioned buying.

"Out of the haze I was in, I heard the old woman telling me that this was in partial payment of a leg-acy…a debt that was owed to Lucille Steele and through her to me." Lance absently set down the packet and dug into his pocket for the ring box. "Lu-cille was my grandmother, but I was focused on the ring, the answer to my prayer. I couldn't have spo-ken…not even if I had been able to think of what to say or the questions I should've asked."

Opening the ring box, he once again gasped at the first sight of the antique ring inside. It took his breath away.

"Anyway," he finally continued with a whoosh of air. "While I studied the intricate carvings and spar-kling diamonds, the gypsy mumbled something like, 'Let this ring take you to your heart's desire.' When I looked up again, the gypsy woman had disap-peared."

He held the open box out for Marcy to see. "Look at this ring. Isn't it spectacular?"

"It's truly beautiful, Lance." Marcy gently fin-gered the ring, and he belatedly realized she was standing right before him.

When he glanced up, she was looking straight at him and not at the ring. Her eyes had turned from light brown to crystallized amber, and they shone with unshed tears like shimmery liquid gold. His hand reached to touch her cheek.

In the depths of her eyes, he saw Christmases yet

to come, all sparkling and bright. With children, babies, warmth and laughter.

"Lance…"

His fingers stroked the satiny softness of her jaw. But when his thumb ran across her bottom lip, the cozy warm emotions changed with lightning intensity.

She leaned into his palm and placed the softest of kisses there. He exploded with need. As she turned to gaze into his eyes, he saw the reflection of his own lust on her face. Their warmth had ignited in an agony of fire.

He blinked. Once. Twice. As beautiful as she was, and as much as he wanted her, *this* wasn't the woman for him. Deciding that what he'd seen in her eyes was an illusion born of simple desire, Lance backed away and broke the connection.

"I…I'm going…out," he stammered. "I have some chores to do, so I'll be gone for quite a while. Don't worry about me." With a loud snap he closed the ring box, turned to the door…and ran.

Eight

Marcy's feet seemed glued to the floor as she stared at the empty space where Lance had stood only moments before. Her nerves still hummed with need. Her body still flamed at all the spots where he'd touched her skin.

What happened? She wrapped her arms around her middle, hugging back the cold, empty loneliness that his sudden departure caused.

That was twice, now, that they'd been close to fulfilling what had become her urgent dream. Twice that he'd pushed away and left her standing, arms aching to hold him and lips tingling for more of his kisses.

This time, though, she had actually felt the magic in the air. The sizzle of it continued to pulsate around her.

She tried swallowing down the desire, but that

didn't do much to alleviate her needs. Spinning around in a circle, Marcy fought to steady herself.

A baby's cry crept through the purple haze that surrounded her. Angie. The baby needed her, and she shook herself free from the sensual fog to go to her daughter's side. She wanted Lance as much as the baby needed her, and she wondered what she could do differently to keep him with her the next time?

He had to want her as much as she wanted him, she was absolutely positive. So maybe it was up to her to get around his indecision. Running a hand through her mass of unruly hair, Marcy vowed to find a way to make a difference.

Somehow, she would make him understand that there was nothing she expected from him. In fact, a commitment to stay in one place with one person was the very last thing on her mind. He could go back to Montana and build a home after she was gone. But they just *had* to find out where this electric tension between them would lead before they went their separate ways.

Marcy changed the baby, carried her to the kitchen and plopped her into the high chair Lance had dragged down from the attic. "I think I just need to fix myself up to look sexier. Don't you agree, Angie?"

The baby grinned as Marcy went about pouring some milk and opening a jar of baby food. "I'm sure he likes me well enough, so that isn't a problem," she told her child. "I bet it's just that he has a little of that motherhood thing your daddy had."

Angie babbled as Marcy took her time sitting down

in a kitchen chair beside her and then picked up the baby food jar. Unintelligible words and sounds came spewing from the baby's mouth as she reached out to her mother.

"Oh, it isn't about you, sweetheart," Marcy crooned as she spooned the food into Angie's waiting mouth. "I know he likes you, too. I've caught him staring at you when he wasn't aware I was watching. There's a special tenderness in his eyes when he looks at you that's clear enough for anyone to understand." The baby grinned again, and food went dribbling over her chin.

Marcy took a halfhearted swipe at the mess and tried once more. "It's that shadow of something wild and slightly dangerous in his eyes when he looks at me that I have to find out more about." Marcy shivered as the memory of his touch danced down her spine and landed, wet and heavy, at the base. "Let's make the kitchen and great room feel like a real Christmas for him, Angie. Then I'll see if I can find a way to become sexy enough so he won't be able to stop the next time. Okay?"

Angie giggled and rocked back and forth in her chair. Marcy took it as a good sign that her daughter agreed with all her mother's decisions.

After giving the baby a cup of milk and cleaning off her face and hands, she put Angie on the kitchen floor with a couple of pots and pans and a big serving spoon so she could play and make all the noise she wanted. They were going to have fun. Marcy hadn't made Christmas decorations since she was little.

While she kept an eye on Angie, she baked tons of

cookie dough snowmen, a Santa and all his reindeer. Vicki kept red and green sugar sprinkles in her pantry so the decorations turned out quite festive.

Then Marcy found a box of aluminum foil. Digging into the recesses of her memory, she remembered how her mother had built shiny silver ornaments out of foil. Sparkly aluminum stars, balls, snowflakes and even an angel.

When Marcy was finished, the kitchen and great room had homemade ornaments hanging from every surface. She found a couple of candles and made a pretty table centerpiece. The place smelled of cinnamon and sugar, and everything looked warm and cozy, resembling a real old-fashioned Christmas.

She hoped that Lance would like what she'd done.

Thinking of Lance, she wondered if he was all right outside. It had been a couple of hours since he'd left, and she hadn't heard a thing from him. If only the windows were clear, perhaps she could spot him as he worked nearby.

"I wonder if the attic has a window," she murmured to Angie as she swung her up in her arms. "Let's go check it out."

Marcy and the baby climbed the stairs to the second-floor attic and opened a big door at the top. The one large and open room had finished walls, a wood floor and a dormer window at one end. Enough filtered light streamed through the glass so that she could see well enough.

As Marcy made her way around boxes and furniture and headed for the window, she realized that Vicki and Bobby were a lot neater about their stored things than most people she knew. The boxes were all marked and stacked in sections. And the furniture was arranged in such a way that Marcy was sure their children used this space as a playroom.

Finally she stood at the window with Angie in her arms, looking out to the north over a wide expanse of yard. The landscape was flat and covered in icy blue snow for as far as she could see. Shadows of evergreens, half-buried in the stark white, could be seen peeking out in patches here and there.

Tiny icicles hung off the roof and made her think of outdoor Christmas decorations. It was late afternoon and the rose and violet rays of refracted sun bounced off the ice with gay abandon. The world outside was a winter wonderland.

Looking closer, she noticed a set of footprints in the snow, leading out of her line of sight. One lonely set of prints going out but none coming back.

He'd told her not to worry. So she tried to think of something else.

With Angie in her arms, she turned back to the cozy attic room. As she did, Marcy spied large black plastic bags stashed in a corner and seeming out of place in the neat space.

When she got close enough to see, a plainly printed note that was pinned to the top bag came into view. "Look at that, Angie," she said absently. "These are old clothes that they've bagged up to send to charity. Most of the things are baby clothes their children must've grown out of. See? The bags are marked with children's ages.''

One of the bags near the top was labeled Girl—Twelve to Eighteen Months.

"You don't suppose Vicki would mind if we went through the clothes?" Marcy asked the baby. "Maybe some of these things will fit you."

She went through the top bag and found two pair of pants and a sweater that fit Angie. Then she came across an adorable red dress with white fake fur trim in the shape of Christmas trees that was only slightly big on the baby. "This will be fun for you to wear tonight when Lance comes back, Angie."

The baby gurgled and patted Marcy's cheek. "Ma…Ma."

Laughing and jiggling her baby in her arms, Marcy hugged her tight. "You said real words, Angie. How about that."

But just then the bag directly underneath the little girl's clothes caught her attention. It was marked in a way that made Marcy think it must be Vicki's outgrown or out-of-date things. She opened it up and found dressy dresses and shoes, a few fancy sweaters and a couple of satiny robes.

Holding her breath, Marcy pulled out a slinky black dress with sparkly rhinestones sewn in the material. She'd never seen anything so beautiful and…sexy.

When she held it up to herself, she couldn't help the smile that came. "I think it's going to fit just fine. Now we can fix up for a real Christmas Eve party, baby. Let's go take a long bubble bath and make ourselves pretty."

By the time she heard Lance at the mudroom door, Marcy had languished for a half hour in a perfumed bath, then dressed both herself and the baby in their fancy clothes. Her own mass of frizzy curls was pinned up and almost sophisticated, while Angie's baby-fine wisps were held back tenuously with a foil-covered bobby pin.

The spaghetti dinner was cooking on the stove and everything was in place for their Christmas Eve party. She ran a hand down to smooth out the wrinkles of the white apron she'd put over the black dress. Throwing her shoulders back, she went to see what was taking Lance so long at the door.

But she couldn't get close to the mudroom. "What on earth is this?" she asked.

From behind a bushy pine tree that was taking up most of the space in the mudroom, Lance sounded rough but strong. "It's a Christmas tree. Just wait until we get it set up, it's a beauty."

"But where did you buy a tree? How did you get to a store?"

"Buy? No way," Lance said as he came into view behind the tree. "Bobby has a stand of evergreens on the back section of his land. I cut the tree myself. And now if you'll fill this bucket with water, I'll get it set up in the great room."

She did as he asked, and within a few minutes the tree was installed and ready to be trimmed. Together, she and Lance took down some of the aluminum balls and strings of popcorn and used them to decorate the tree. The smell of fresh-cut pine added to the cozy ambience and was just the thing to make the place seem ready for Christmas.

"It's beautiful," she said as she stepped back to admire the tree and took off her apron. "What made you think of it?"

"I've never had a Christmas tree before. And when I saw the pine trees, I just thought it might make Christmas a little more special for you and Angie this year." He turned a full circle, taking in the whole place, then stopped as his gaze lazily wandered up her body and back to her feet again. "But the decorations and tree are not the only beautiful and special things here. What have you done to yourself? You look—" he cleared his throat "—terrific."

She raised a hand to pat down a wayward curl that had escaped the pins, and tried a smile. "Angie and I found some things in the attic that Vicki had set aside for donation. I hope she doesn't mind that we tried them on." Twisting around so he could see the back of her dress, Marcy felt her nerves singing under his scrutiny. "Do you like it?"

He stepped closer and gently pushed another curl behind her ear. "You look like a million bucks. I wish I *could* get to a store right now. Sparkling earrings would make the outfit complete." His fingers lingered against her earlobe, softly rubbing the tender skin there. "On the other hand, you don't need fancy stones to make you more beautiful. You are a brilliant gem…a shining diamond…all on your own."

It was the nicest thing anyone had ever said to her. She bit back the tears that threatened and stepped out of his reach. "Thank you. I hope you're hungry, because Angie and I made you a special Christmas dinner. She's waiting for you to begin."

Marcy took his arm and pulled him toward the kitchen. "Don't forget to compliment her on her new outfit," she whispered. "Angie's never had such a pretty dress before and she needs your approval."

"You two did all this…" He waved his hand through the air. "The decorations, the dinner, the dresses. For me?"

"We wanted you to know we're sorry you had to miss your Christmas Eve party back in Montana," Marcy told him. "And the look on your face was worth all the work."

Lance swallowed hard to force away his suddenly blurred vision, then made a big fuss over Angie's new dress. "Can you ladies wait a few more minutes while I take a quick shower?" he finally asked. "I'm too grubby to be seen with two such gorgeous women."

Besides, he thought, if he didn't take a moment, he would never be able to get through supper.

After the dishes were washed and the leftover cookies were put away, he carried a sleepy-eyed Angie to her crib. Marcy got the baby ready for the night while he stoked the fire in the great room and found an orchestral Christmas CD to play.

The tree, the decorations and the carols all combined to put him in a mellow mood by the time Marcy joined him on the sofa in front of the fire. "You did a wonderful job with everything," he told her. "I'm sure the Christmas Eve party in Montana is not nearly this cozy."

In the flickering light of the fire, he saw her flush with pleasure at his words. The pink stain moved to her neck and spread across her shoulders. It was almost more than he could stand to keep himself from wrapping her up in his arms so he could let his lips follow that flush to all her tender places.

The slinky dress she'd chosen fit her like a second skin. Black and shimmery against her pale complexion, the dress made her look sexy as hell. It also made him wonder what she had on underneath.

"I talked to one of Bobby and Vicki's neighbors this afternoon," he said instead of doing what his body was beginning to demand. "Stan Ottwell. He was on his snowmobile and saw me cutting down the tree."

"Oh? Was he upset?"

"Naw. I've met Stan before. I told him what happened to us and why we're here. He said he'd heard that the highway had been reopened this morning and that the snowplows would be out working by tomorrow." Lance watched Marcy's eyes widened and turn to golden amber once again. "He also offered to bring his tractor over tomorrow afternoon after Christmas dinner and dig the SUV out of the ditch."

"So soon?" She scooted closer to him and the heat from the fireplace exploded in his gut.

"Yeah," he mumbled. "Looks like we'll get you and Angie to Cheyenne in plenty of time." Lance opened and closed his fists, trying to relieve the pressure of the building flames that burned him from the inside out.

Stretching his shoulder blades, he attempted to move away from her sensual draw. "Man, my shoul-

LINDA CONRAD 127

ders are sure stiff from using that saw today. Guess I'm out of practice.''

Marcy kicked off her shoes and knelt on the sofa beside him. ''Turn your back. I'll massage the muscles.''

Slowly turning, he shook his head at his stupidity. Sore muscles, what a stupid excuse. Another bad idea.

She began to knead his shoulders, and every place she touched erupted in fire. Yep. *Really* bad idea.

''Uh, Marcy...''

Her hands gentled, slowed and moved down his arms. The atmosphere in the great room shifted, thickened and intensified until it became heavy and alive with hunger. It smelled of pine and vanilla...and desire. And to Lance it felt like an end to reserve and the beginning of surrender.

She pulled the rawhide thong from his hair, pushed aside the freed strands and placed her lips against the back of his neck as she leaned her breasts into his back. He could feel her nipples harden against him. The very air was electrified with arousal.

He had to back away before his every good intention was lost, but he couldn't bear to see her hurt expression one more time. Standing, he turned to face her and held out his hand. ''Dance with me.''

With a surprised look, she slowly nodded and joined him. Moving into his arms, Marcy sighed when he pulled her close. He guided them in a slow waltz while the CD played a soft and melancholy Christmas tune. But as they moved together, he lost track of what he'd meant to do.

Her body melded to his. Soft to hard. Two separate needs, blending in time to the music.

Bending his head, he kissed her temple and caught a whiff of that sexy, sunshine smell. She moaned against his chest, suddenly reminding him of his vow and stirring him to action. He stepped back and broke his hold on her.

She lifted her chin, and the disappointment and confusion were clear in her eyes. "Is it me?" she whispered. "I don't know what I'm doing wrong. Is it because I'm a mother that I turn you off?"

"What?" The pain on her face drove an unbearable ache deep into his chest. "I think we'd better talk, Marcy." He put his arm around her shoulders and guided her to the sofa.

After they were settled, he decided to begin right away before she started to imagine the worst. "Where on earth would you get the idea that you're doing anything wrong? You couldn't possibly do one thing that would be considered even remotely wrong, and I respect you more than I can say."

"But…"

He lifted a finger and placed it against her lips. "Let me finish. You're a wonderful mother. I can't imagine anyone doing a better job." She dropped her chin so he used a thumb and forefinger to gently lift it again. "Listen, please. You've faced adversity with grace and good humor. Not many people, men or women, would've gone through what you have without whining. And you never complained once.

"You're a special person, Marcy. You've found a way to take care of your daughter and go after what you want in life. I admire you for it. It's taken me a lot of years to decide to try for what I want.''

Her eyes met his gaze and the air sizzled with hot promise. "Then why…why don't I…interest you… physically?" she stammered.

He let himself touch her face…to soothe her…to satisfy him. "You know I want you. I think you have to be the sexiest woman I've ever known. And you must feel the electricity in the air whenever we touch." Right this minute the tension was about to explode all around them. "But we want different things. This isn't a game. We'll be going our separate ways in a day or two. I don't want…"

It was Marcy's turn to place a finger against his lips. "I know all that. But *I* don't want a long-term relationship the same as you do." She smiled at him and his brain went south. "I'm not saying that I fall into bed with every man who, uh, makes me feel special. In fact, only one man has ever been in my bed. But you have to admit there is something out of the ordinary between us, and we need to explore what that is before it's too late."

She laid a hand against his chest, and his heart thudded. "See there. See how you react when I touch you? My whole body does that whenever you're in the same room."

Leaning in, she placed a light kiss on his lips. "Please, Lance. Please let us find out if this is really magic. Give me a chance."

The fire crackled as the sparks he'd tried to bury ignited in the sultry depths of his gut. The lines he'd drawn began to combust, while flames burned through the balance of control and resolve blew away in a puff of smoke.

Cupping her cheek with one hand, he slid the other to the nape of her neck to hold her head steady as he gently explored the sweetness of her mouth. She tasted of hot chocolate and cinnamon, and he got carried away on a scent of sunshine and vanilla. With a final sigh, he released himself from his vows of chastity and made new vows.

He pulled a pin from her hair and flexed his fingers, itching to run them through all that silky softness. "Your hair looks nice. But I think I'd rather it was down."

She raised her eyebrows, then smiled shyly before helping him remove the pins. Shaking her hair out in a fluffy blond cloud around her head, she stood up and laughed. "And I think you have on way too many clothes."

He was quick to his feet, this man she'd set her sights on having. Folding her into his arms, he covered her lips with a determined and passionate kiss. Surprise and a tiny spurt of panic shot through her veins as his mouth captured hers with heat and power.

Hunger met hunger, and passion tangled with desire. He slanted his mouth across hers, then tugged at her lower lip, begging to deepen the kiss. Opening for him, her tongue found his in an exquisite dance of fire.

Barely able to breathe, her hands moved up his shoulders and into ebony strands of hair. He dipped his tongue inside her mouth, tasting, exploring, tantalizing. Arching closer, she felt the tips of her nipples grow hard and sensitive as they pressed against his chest.

Her whole body grew heavy and achy with desire as he groaned softly and drove his fingers through her hair. Suddenly it was urgent that she see him. Tugging wildly at his shirt, she pulled it from the waistband of his jeans and tried unbuttoning it with shaky hands.

Lance covered her hands with his own and, leaning back with a wry grin, he helped her to free him from the chambray. He shrugged out of the shirt and pitched it over his shoulder. Blinking back the shock of seeing his expanse of golden-bronze skin gleaming in the firelight, Marcy stood whimpering and gaping in amazement at the broad shoulders and rippling biceps.

He was beyond her wildest and sexiest fantasies. The one other man of her experience paled both literally and figuratively in comparison.

But Lance didn't give her long to admire his physique. He reached for her, and kissed her with such a combination of reverence and lust that it nearly broke her heart.

Without breaking the kiss, she reached for his hand and placed it against her breast, trying desperately to find a way to soothe the aching tenderness there. It was his turn to whimper as his knuckles brushed against her bare skin.

He hooked his thumbs under her dress's spaghetti straps while dangerous, mindless sensations drove her over an edge. She let the thin pieces of material slide down her arms. His eyes flamed and his nostrils flared as he watched her wiggle, letting the dress slither down her body.

With every nerve ending alive and on fire, Marcy stepped out of the dress and fought the urge to cover her breasts with her hands. Instead she kept her arms at her sides and allowed him to look all he wanted.

She hadn't worn a bra, and now all she had to cover her nakedness was the flimsy material of her cheap see-through panties. But she didn't feel as if she'd done anything wrong or naughty. In fact, the way that Lance's gaze lazily wandered over her body made her stand up taller and revel in the warm, passionate vibrations he was sending her way.

But looking simply wasn't enough. When she moved toward him, he captured her in his embrace and began kissing every inch of skin that had just been under his gaze.

Stirring the bewitched potion of shared desire by licking and touching, he began to drive her up a steep and slippery slope. She was headed toward a place that had only lived in her imagination before.

She knew he had the power to take her there and, in her frantic need, willed him to hurry it up. Wrapping her arms around his neck, Marcy tasted desire right through his skin—and hung on for a lifetime ride to the stars.

Nine

"**E**asy," he murmured. "Easy, there." He pulled back and tried gentling them both the way he would a skittish colt.

But gentle wasn't what his body cried out for. And gentle didn't seem to be what Marcy had in mind.

His heart stumbled when she threw him an intimate look and a teasing smile. Her sensuality robbed him of breath and left him wallowing in intoxicating passion.

Reaching out, he dragged her into his embrace as he lasered a kiss across those full, pink lips. He was lost in the drugging sensation of her hands, moving rhythmically up and down his bare arms. Running his hands over her body in return, he tested her most sensitive places.

When he covered a breast and flicked a thumb over

the hardened nipple, she cried out, thrusting against his hand. Her breasts fit perfectly in his palms. He bent to lave and nip the rosy nubs and watched in fascination as they peaked and beaded under the touch of his tongue.

Biting back the urgent demands of his body, he silently vowed to hold down his needs and let her take pleasure in their mating. Her hands roamed downward toward the waistband of his jeans and he found himself repeating that vow like a commandment.

But then she pressed a palm against the hardened length straining behind his fly, and the vow disintegrated as he heard himself groaning into her ear. Frantically he sucked on earlobes, fingers and nipples. Any sensitive body part he could reach.

When her fingers slipped beneath his waistband, the heat scorched what was left of his mind. He ground his mouth down hungrily on her slightly parted lips.

She ran a finger over the slick, moist tip of his erection and he stopped thinking and breathing altogether. Both blind with need and impatient with desire, the two of them tore at his zipper. A moment later the jeans had joined his shirt on the floor, and she was stroking his throbbing flesh and cradling him in her hands.

A sharp, intense pinch of pleasure bulleted through him. He closed his eyes and clung to her as she cupped him, letting curious fingers roam across ridges and slide down valleys of his arousal. Mind-shattering and erotic as hell, he felt himself grow with blissful satisfaction.

When he could stand no more and his breath was coming in short static bursts, he pulled out of her grasp. Driving his fingers beneath the elastic of her panties, he slid them down her legs and she stepped out of them.

He knelt before her and reverently pressed his lips against her belly. She moaned and her knees buckled, so he filled his hands with her buttocks and held her to him.

As he tasted her salty, sensitive skin and ringed her navel with his tongue, she mewled, and her shivers of pleasure rocked through them both. He bent to nibble the tender skin along the insides of her thighs, finally pressing a worshiping kiss against the baby-fine blond hair covering her inner core.

She trembled and dug her fingernails into his shoulders, urging him to hurry.

"Easy," he mumbled once more. And this time, he had himself somewhat under control. "We have all night to make this right. Let me make it good for you."

She groaned and, with one fast scoop, he reached under her knees and flipped her over his shoulder. He'd thought he might make it to a bed. But his own knees were so shaky they wouldn't hold him. So he released her to collapse back on the sofa.

Gasping, her knees fell apart as she tried to sit up. He didn't give her an instant to catch her breath or her balance as he crawled between her thighs, pinning her exactly where he wanted.

Moving close, he ran a hand up her leg and on up her rib cage, finally letting his fingers play with a nipple. Meanwhile, he bent his head to her hot, wet sex and used the other hand to open her to his lips. She squirmed with every touch against her most sensitive skin.

While he pleasured her nub with his clever tongue, he eased a finger inside her core and felt the inner muscles clench around him. He heard her gasp and call his name. Her moans encouraged him to increase the in-and-out friction of both tongue and fingers.

She writhed and moaned incoherently but he held her fast. Ignoring his own needs, he drew her up to a fevered frenzy, then slowed the pace and gentled his touch to drive her wild.

"Lance. Lance." Marcy screamed and grabbed handfuls of his hair. "I need...I need...please...I don't know how," she begged.

He wanted to make her forget every other encounter she'd had. At the same time, he wanted her to remember this time—and him—forever. Nudging her higher again, he began to realize that no one had ever made her this wild, this hot, this frantic.

His ego swelled with his arousal, but his body's demands suddenly took control. "I don't have protection," he gasped as he pulled her tightly against him.

"It's all right." She breathed in his ear. "The doctor put me on the pill to even out my hormones." Her voice trembled with desire and her breathing was ragged.

"Right," he choked as he grabbed the afghan off

the back of the sofa and spread it on the floor in front of the fire. "I wanted to make you crazy with desire."

He slid her to the floor and into his needy arms. "But I can't wait…" he whispered in a jagged voice. "Dammit. I just can't…"

His mouth covered hers while he pressed her back to the soft afghan. The passion captured him with such a powerful force, it was like nothing he'd ever experienced.

Running his hands down her rib cage then sliding them under her bottom, they lay together as if they had been made from the same mold. Woman-man.

"Lance," she urged.

He knew she was close. So was he. And though he wanted to drag this out—to feast forever on her perfection—it was just too intense.

Planting his palms beside her head and nudging her open, he plunged with ferocious need. Marcy raised her hips to take him higher, and he almost blacked out from the sensation. He was a goner now. Untamed, raw and savage. He thrust uncontrollably.

Her muscles began to contract around him. From somewhere out of his drugged haze, he heard her breathy moans spiraling higher.

"Oh, oh, oh," she screamed.

He stilled with a supreme effort and ground against her as her climax smashed into them both. On and on it went, with wave after wave of pleasure. Her body's reaction shattered him like shards of brittle glass, prickling at his own need and driving him to a higher passion-filled plain.

As the sweet circles of her climax moved to the

edges of his body, he began pumping into that ocean of warmth with everything he had. She wrapped her legs around his waist and raised her hips to meet him thrust for thrust.

Sucking in one sharp, final breath, he lowered his head and slanted a desperate kiss across her mouth. The white-hot climax hit him with furious fire, branding him with her essence—forever.

It was like nothing that had come before. And deep in his fevered brain, he knew nothing that came after would ever be the same.

Several unconscious moments later, he wrapped her in his embrace and rolled them both over. He held on to her with an uneasy possessiveness.

Sprawled lazily across his chest, she tried to regulate her breathing. "Wow," she gulped. "That was…that was…"

He chuckled at her loss of words and wondered if he could do any better without becoming overly sentimental. But there was something he had to know.

"Yes, it was, wasn't it?" He pressed a gentle kiss to her hair. "Marcy, somewhere in the middle of all that you said that you'd never, uh… Well, it seemed like that was the first time you'd ever, uh…"

"Yes, Lance. That was the first time I'd ever climaxed during sex. It was amazing."

Amazing wasn't the word for it. "But you were married. You have a child." He could feel a rough combination of fury at her ex and sadness that she'd been so alone creeping up to kick him in the gut.

She raised her head and grinned. "You have every

right to beat your chest with pride, Tarzan. What you do to me, what we do together, is special. It really is magical.''

The lump in his throat didn't feel much like magic. ''I sort of wish you hadn't told me,'' he groaned.

She sighed, and her breath ruffled the hair on his chest, stirring his sex to life. He wanted her again. He was deathly afraid that he would always want her.

Marcy ran her fingers down his arm and took a long breath. He had given her the most amazing sexual experience of her entire life. And he'd done it with restrained tenderness. She laid her head against his heart as the racing beat matched her own.

He reached up to brush a damp and wayward curl from her forehead. They were both sticky with sweat and the remnants of their passion, but she couldn't care less.

They had been wild for each other. Yet, she knew he had held himself back. Probably he'd been afraid of hurting her somehow. He didn't know how tough she was...or how badly she wanted to unleash the full power that she knew raged between them. Well, she had at least one more day.

There were a couple of things she had to say to him, as well. Things she wanted him to know before they walked away from each other for good.

But now wasn't the time. She shivered when the thought of walking away landed firmly in her mind.

''You cold?'' he asked. ''Give me a minute to build up the fire and get us a couple more blankets.''

''Are we sleeping out here?'' The dumb question came out of her mouth before she thought to keep it to herself, but she'd never considered sleeping on the floor when they had perfectly good beds in the house.

"Do you mind?" He dragged her up and into his lap. "I promise not to let you get too cold," he said with a teasing leer.

Marcy studied his beautiful face in the firelight. Behind that wry grin was a mixture of sadness and passion. The combination was confusing and compelling. She cupped his stubbled chin and softly placed her lips to his.

"I wouldn't want to be anywhere else in the world tonight," she whispered against his mouth and surprised herself by meaning every word. "But I need to go check on Angie first and make sure she'll be okay until morning."

He nodded once and brought them both up to stand on shaky feet. "Don't take too long," he said right before he clamped his mouth down on hers and took her breath away.

When she finally stepped out of his embrace and headed for the guest room, her heart was thumping madly in her chest. One of the things she would not be telling him, was how much she'd come to care. She knew she was slipping over the ragged edge to full-blown love, and the last thing she wanted to do was to make things difficult for him by letting him know.

Angie was sleeping peacefully in her crib. Marcy rubbed her hand across the fine down of hair on her child's head and whispered a little prayer. Nothing in her life was as important as her baby daughter. Nothing had been, that is, until Lance walked into their lives.

She made sure the temperature in the baby's room was warm enough and that there were no loose things in the crib. Then she made her way into the guest bathroom to splash some cold water over her face.

When she flipped on the overhead light, she stared at the naked woman she saw looking back at her in the full-length mirror. Her eyes were glazed and sultry, her breasts still taut and high. She ran a finger over full, plump lips that had turned beet red from Lance's caresses.

It turned her on to see what a wild woman she'd become under his tutoring. She picked up a brush and tried to run it through the tangle of curls on her head, but ended up just pinning them off her neck instead.

With her arms raised to her hair, she was fully exposed when Lance appeared behind her in the mirror. She stilled, watching his eyes darken and narrow as they raked over her form in the mirror.

A shot of pure adrenaline pushed through her, fast and dangerously reckless, as she looked at their reflections together in the mirror. Dark and light. Night and day. The contrast was ying and yang, power and glory. It nearly swept her off her feet with need.

Silently he stepped closer to her back while her breasts throbbed and her heart lay like a lump in her throat. He bent and placed his lips against her neck, sending goose bumps cascading along her heated body and wetness to the place between her legs.

He spread his warm golden hand wide on her lower abdomen and pulled her bottom tightly against his groin. The feel of his full erection, hot and heavy against her back, sent electric jolts of erotic sensation directly to the base of her spine and she nearly fainted. Light-headed with desire, but hesitant to move and break the spell, she moaned and let her head fall back against his chest.

"No, honey," he whispered in her ear. "Open your eyes and watch."

Dazed but determined to do as he asked, Marcy propped open her heavy lids. Her gaze met his in the mirror and she gasped as she saw the dangerous passion in his eyes. She felt weak and limp, but he held her fast.

With his free hand, he began rubbing his palm over her chest and up her neck. "Look what happens to your body when I do this," he said as his fingers tugged gently on her nipples.

He lightly pinched first one and then the other, and she saw her nipple react, growing rosy red and beading against his fingers. His touch grew stronger and more insistent until the tips of her breasts were so sensitive she found herself breathing in little gasps and the pull of arousal had become an agony of pleasure.

But he didn't let up and kept encouraging her to watch them in the mirror. The hand on her belly moved lower, and his fingers slid through the curls of her mound. When he found the place that cried out for him, she saw her own eyes grow wide as the shock of his touch jolted through her. Her hips bucked back against him and he groaned against her ear.

"Keep your eyes open and let go," he urged.

"It's too much," she sobbed.

Reaching up behind her head, she grabbed handfuls of his hair, pulling him closer. He licked her earlobe and blew lightly against it, sending chills down her body to compete with the heat moving up from where his thumbs kept steadily rubbing and massaging both her breasts and her most tender nub.

"Now, honey," he said softly. "Now."

The shattering quakes of climax hit her without warning. Her arms and legs trembled and she saw herself cry out when the flood of warmth careened over her. She tried to keep her eyes open but shooting stars blinded her to everything but the pulsing sizzle of sensations.

Her blood was still boiling in her veins as he urged her to lean over the counter. Close behind her, he used a hand on her inner thigh, stroking and rubbing until she involuntarily widened her stance.

She felt his hard arousal nudge and probe the opening to her depths. "Yes," she moaned. "Now, Lance."

Her urgent pleading seemed to stir him as he pushed the tip of his sex against her throbbing core. He grabbed her hips and, bending over her back, placed wet branding kisses on her shoulders.

The heat moved down from where he kissed and landed in her belly. When he bit into her neck, holding her in place with his mouth, she felt herself heading for the edge again. "Please," she said in a voice she didn't recognize.

With a powerful lunge, he plunged into her on one

long silky glide. He growled, low and deep in his chest.

Lance was beyond thinking, beyond demand and past civilization. Sweat ran down his temple, over his shoulders and down his spine with the formidable effort it had taken to watch her come apart in the mirror.

When she groaned, writhed against his groin and sobbed his name, all was lost in a savage momentum. He was gloved tightly inside her fire and could feel her internal muscles gripping and stroking his sex. Her body was pulling him to completion.

They were both groaning, making feral animal sounds, as he held her steady with his mouth on her shoulder and his palm tightly against her mound. The next thrust went deeper. Marcy cursed and pushed her hips against him again.

His hips slammed against her bottom as thrust after thrust drove them both frantically nearer a peak. Her tight muscles clenched and sucked at him with every movement.

He could feel himself nearing the end, so he slid his hand down to where they were joined and stroked her nub with a jerking movement. Marcy stilled, gasped, then shattered as the bubbling culmination swamped her.

The vibrations beat against him as she shook and cried. That was all it took to push him over the highest cliff. With one last thrust, his own crest overtook then claimed him with shooting sparks and a lava flow of incandescent warmth.

It took him a long time to come to his senses. His knees were weak and the quakes were still echoing through them both. He gently pulled away from her and turned her into his arms.

''Are you all right?'' he murmured and kissed her temple.

Wrapping her arms tightly around his neck, she kissed him back. ''Oh, yes,'' she whispered against his lips. ''I'm better than all right. I'm the best.''

''Yes, you are,'' he grinned. ''And that time there were two.''

''Two?''

''Yep. Wanna go for three?''

''You...you're counting,'' she groaned as the pink flame rose over her chest and up her neck.

''I said I wished you hadn't told me.''

''Lance, this is not a competition.''

He laughed, really laughed, for what might've been the first time in his life and pulled her close. ''No, maybe not, but you are such a joy to tease.'' Placing a tender kiss on her shoulder, he whispered against her skin. ''I love to watch your skin flame from my words...and my touch. I love to see how your eyes glaze over when you're about to reach the heights. And I can't stop wanting you, all the time.''

Moaning, she lowered her forehead to his shoulder. He bent to nibble on her neck when he spotted a mark on her skin that shook him. ''Hell.''

She drew back and gazed at him with a question in her eyes. Kicking himself six ways from Sunday, he scooped her up and took both of them into the tub.

''I left a mark on you,'' he muttered under his breath as he turned on the tap and regulated the water's temperature. ''A bite mark. Dammit.''

"But…" She reached up and ran her hand over the spot on her neck. "You didn't break the skin. It's fine."

He turned on the shower and let her slide down his body so she could stand under the spray. But he kept a hand around her waist, needing the connection.

Marcy gasped when the water sluiced down over her head. She giggled and rotated in Lance's embrace, turning her back to the water and her front to his chest.

"We were wild, weren't we?" she asked dreamily.

Lance scowled and narrowed his eyes while he inspected her neck and soaped up his hands. "I can't believe I bruised you. I must've lost my mind."

"I think we both lost our minds." She raised a hand and touched the many fingernail scratches across his shoulders. "But it's the way I wanted it, Lance. I wouldn't have let you do anything that didn't feel good."

He ran his soapy hand lightly over her shoulders and up her neck. Then putting a finger under her chin, he raised her face and gently touched her lips with his own.

"That's all I want," he murmured as his other hand slid soap over her breasts. "I don't ever want to hurt you, honey. I just want to make you feel good. Special. The same way you do for me."

A reply stuck in her throat. With a strangled gurgle she rubbed her soapy, sensitive breasts against his chest and breathed in the wicked scents of lavender soap and masculine desire.

The need rose in them both once more. Her blood

heated as the hot shower spray beat down on their bodies and steam rose up to envelop them in a sensual fog.

His hands touched her everywhere. Fondling, massaging, kneading her into a frenzy.

She tried to climb right inside him and wrapped her legs around his waist. Pressing her back against the cool tile, he entered her in one swift movement. The liquid fire raced along her skin as she trembled and tightened around him.

She shuddered while her climax pulsed through them both. He kissed her desperately and drove deeper, intensifying the pleasure.

Higher they climbed, fast and furious with exquisite jolts pushing them onward. Once more, then once again, the rolls of fulfillment crashed through her until at last Lance shuddered and followed.

She tried to remember how to breathe as she sagged against him. He slowly lowered her until her feet touched the tub floor. Then he turned off the water and bundled them both in huge towels. Groggy and shaken, she let Lance carry her back to the blankets in front of the fire and settle them both down for the night.

A baby's high-pitched squeal woke her from a sensual dream. Rolling over, she reached for Lance, but her hand touched nothing except blankets.

She'd awakened several times during the night with the sensation of his hot mouth covering her breast. She'd never felt so sensual, so needed. They turned to each other over and over, seeking warmth and finding the sizzle of breathtaking desire.

Blinking open her eyes, she found the flames roaring in the fireplace above her. He must've stoked the fire when he'd gotten up. But where was he now?

She decided she'd better get up herself and see about Angie. As Marcy stirred, delicious aches throbbed in muscles and places that were long forgotten. Smiling to herself at the memories of how she'd come by those aches, she stood and pulled a blanket around her shoulders.

When she looked down at the sofa, expecting to find a tangle of their discarded clothes from last night, she saw instead a soft pink chenille robe folded neatly with a note on the top. The note was from Lance.

It said, "I'm not positive this will fit, but the color is the same color your skin becomes when you blush. Try it on and come join the party. Merry Christmas, honey."

Ten

Marcy shrugged into the soft robe and sighed with pleasure. Burying her nose in the baby-pink material at her shoulder, she took a whiff and knew immediately that this was not a hand-me-down. She'd never owned anything this nice that was also brand-new.

Another high-pitched squeal, one she recognized as Angie's, caught her attention and drew her toward the kitchen. When she stepped closer, the sight that greeted her made her stop and shake her head.

Lance stood with his back to her at the stove, jiggling a giggling Angie with one hand and stirring something in a pot with the other. It was a picture Marcy had never thought she'd see. A man caring for and about her child.

What a special person he was. She was sure she'd never met anyone like him. Finding herself fighting off the welling tears, Marcy forced her legs to carry her to his side as she swallowed hard and cleared her throat.

"Good morning, you two," she said in a ragged voice.

He turned and grinned. "Ah. Good morning, sleepyhead." Dropping the spoon on the counter, he beckoned her to come close with his free hand.

His ebony eyes were dancing with good humor, but behind the smile she caught a hint of burning passion still lingering in his gaze. He had on a T-shirt and jeans that were riding low on his hips. Her heart began beating in a staccato rhythm. From a foot away she could feel the heated vibrations coming from his athletic body and racing across her nerves.

She stepped into his embrace and got carried away in jumbled sensations. The scent of man and morning-after passion hit her as he pulled her close. She turned her face into his chest and let him hug her tight. The images of what they'd done together left her feeling sexy and desired.

But other sensations were bombarding her with different images and needs at the same time. Angie was babbling away, as happy and content with him as she would be with her mother. And that was such a foreign feeling, it was making Marcy's knees weak with a longing she could barely name.

"I see you found your Christmas present," he said while he placed a tender kiss on the top of her head. "It's a little big, but it looks great on you, just like I'd hoped."

She bit her lip, trying to hold back the overwhelming emotions and gather her wits in order to speak. "Oh, Lance, I can't thank you enough. It's beautiful. I love it," she managed at last. "But where... how..."

He released her and turned back to the pot on the stove. "It was no big deal. A clothing sales rep was stuck with us at the truck stop. I talked him out of a sample, that's all."

"You bought me a present way back at the truck stop?"

"When I saw the color of that robe, I just knew it would be perfect for you," he mumbled. "Plus, I figured you probably didn't have one as warm as that and you might need it on your travels."

That did it. Marcy had to move away from him while she sniffled and choked back the tears. No one had ever done anything so nice for her.

"The oatmeal is ready," Lance said from behind her. "Can you put Angie in the high chair while I dish it up?"

Shaking her shoulders to push away the strong emotions rolling through her chest, she took a breath and pulled Angie out of his arm. But when she grasped the baby and took a step, Angie squealed and reached back for Lance.

"I think you've got yourself another fan," Marcy told him with more cheer than she was feeling.

Lance smiled as he carried two bowls to the kitchen table. "Oh, Angie and I have become good buddies."

She settled Angie and sat down. "You dressed her in the red Christmas dress...and changed her... and..." Words failed Marcy once more.

He shrugged and handed the baby her sippy cup. "We're having a Christmas morning party. I figured she would want to look her best." Sitting down at the table next to Marcy, he bent to kiss her cheek. "Sorry about the oatmeal, but there isn't much else in the cupboard. I did try to dress it up, though. I added cinnamon and a few walnuts I found in Vicki's pantry."

"It's fine, Lance. Wonderful, thank you."

"You're welcome." He reached out and ran a finger gently along her jawline and down her neck while he captured her gaze with his passion-filled eyes. "And thank you for giving me a night…that I'll never forget."

She gulped and wondered how on earth she would ever make it through any kind of food without choking on the sobs working their way up her throat. The man was too much. He'd rescued them from the side of the road, missed his party at home to get them safely through the storm and now was jumping through hoops to make it a merry Christmas.

Besides all that, he'd opened her up to a whole new sensual side of herself that she'd completely missed in her life up to now. And he was thanking *her* for the most spectacular night of her life?

He ate a couple of spoonfuls of the oatmeal, then tilted his head to watch Angie. "I fed her a jar of that baby-food stuff before you got up. But she still looks hungry."

Marcy looked at the baby and saw the same warm need for the man in her child's eyes that she was experiencing—at least in *one* respect. "Angie's just feeling left out," she told him. "We're eating and she has to watch."

"Ah." Lance stood up and went to the counter. "Then maybe this will help."

He picked up a tissue-covered item that Marcy hadn't noticed before and handed it to Angie. "Here, baby girl," he crooned. "Merry Christmas."

Angie's eyes got big and round as she stared at whatever was taking up the entire tray of her high chair. Then she looked to her mother for help.

"Angie doesn't know what a present is," Marcy chuckled. "Maybe I'd better help her with the wrapping."

Lance's heart thumped loudly in his chest while he stood watching Angie's face as her mother unwrapped the baby doll he'd bought. The pretty little doll had blond hair and big blue eyes, just like the real baby. The minute he'd seen it in the truck stop store, he had to get it for Angie.

"Oh, Lance." Marcy uncovered the doll and handed it over to her daughter's waiting arms. "Angie's never had a doll before. What a thoughtful thing for you to do."

He shook his head. "I don't know about thoughtful," he hedged. "I just wanted her to have it."

Angie stared at the doll for a long time, then pointed a finger at the doll's nose. "Ba!" she squealed.

"Yes, Angie, that's your baby doll." Marcy's eyes were shining behind her smile.

"Did she say baby? Is she talking?" Lance was surprised and pleased by the look on Angie's face.

"She's trying to talk," Marcy replied. "Yesterday she said 'ma.' I think that means mama…me."

Angie bent her head, placed her lips to the doll's face and made a smacking noise with her mouth.

"Oh, Angie, you kissed the doll," her mother cooed. "How sweet. We're going to have to give her a name. How about we just call her 'baby'?"

The enthralled little girl put her arms around the doll and hugged it. "Ba."

Lance was speechless and needed to move. He picked Angie and doll up in his arms and danced them both around the room.

For the first time in his life, Lance White Eagle Steele felt fragile—as if he were teetering on the sharp edge of a china cup. All he could think was that if one thing ever hurt this innocent child, his anger and the revenge that followed would be boundless.

He knew he would kill to keep anyone from hurting Angie…and that he would die to keep her safe.

Marcy got up and stood on her tiptoes to kiss his cheek. "Well, whatever possessed you to buy Angie her first doll, the baby and I thank you very much."

When she leaned her breast against his arm and he felt her warm breath brush over his skin, a rush of hot desire shot through his gut and mingled there with the warm, happy feelings he'd been having toward the baby. Man, this was confusing.

He stopped for a second and considered the divergent and entirely new sensations. The lust was nothing new. He'd been lusting after Marcy since almost the first moment he'd spotted her out on that freezing, windswept highway. But there was something more here.

Then it occurred to him that this must be what it felt like to have a family. All these sentimental and sensual tingles were exactly what he'd been longing for and wouldn't recognize—the joy of a real home and family of his own.

The next couple of hours whizzed by as he and Marcy played with the baby and then together put her down for a nap. The time was going by too fast and he willed it to slow down so he could memorize and cherish everything. He was not going to settle for anything less than this in his life.

"I'm going to build a home just like this on the ranch," he told Marcy with a sweep of his hand. They were working in the kitchen to clean up and take down the Christmas decorations in preparation for leaving. "This may've been my first Christmas celebration, but it certainly won't be my last."

Marcy set the candle she'd been wrapping on the counter and placed her hand on his forearm. "Lance. I've been meaning to talk to you about something. Now's as good a time as any. Come sit down a second." She sounded serious and a little sad, and it hurt him not to be able to fix whatever was the matter.

He followed her to the table and pulled out a chair so she could sit, then he swung one around backward for himself. "I'm all yours for as long as you need. What's up?"

She folded her hands on the table and stared down

at them. "I want to tell you what I know about marriage," she said without looking up.

Curious but nervous about what she was going to say, he sat down and crossed his arms over the back of the chair so he could lean against it. "Go on."

"My parents married because I was on the way," she said softly. "I'm not sure there was ever any love there. But by the time I was old enough to recognize such things, I'm positive there wasn't.

"It was not a happy place, my home. My father spent a lot of time out of town. And when he was home, he drank and then he yelled. It was almost like…well, actually I'm sure, he drank because he was miserable, saddled with a woman and child he didn't love."

Marcy looked up into his face, and the forlorn look in her eyes nearly doubled him over. "Honey, if this hurts you to talk about it, don't. Don't make yourself so unhappy."

She smiled sadly and shook her head. "This is important. I want you to listen, please."

He nodded once and she continued. "When I was eighteen, a stranger came to our town. He was only a traveling salesman, selling books to the school district and the library. But I thought he was the most charming, the most worldly man in the universe."

Marcy stopped and swallowed. The words seemed to choke her. "He talked to me about all the places he'd been, all the exciting and wonderful spots where he wanted to take me," she continued at last. "I had only known him for a month when he asked me to marry him and go away to see the world. I didn't love him, but I was so eager to leave my home…so wrapped up in the idea of traveling…that I agreed.''

''But I thought you had never traveled,'' he interrupted. ''When we first met, you said you were going to see the world.''

''Yes,'' she said softly. ''What a big joke that whole marriage turned out to be. Only, the joke was on me. He took me as far as Minneapolis then told me I needed to work and save money so I could travel with him…someday.

''I was surprised, but I agreed. I thought it would be a temporary setback.'' Marcy closed her eyes and took a deep breath. ''Everything went downhill from there. But that's a long sad story you don't need to hear. The point I'm trying to make is that marrying someone you don't love…for any reason…is just plain wrong.''

''Marcy…'' He didn't know what to say to her, but his heart was aching.

She rolled her shoulders and stood up. ''I call it 'soul loneliness.' It's that emptiness you feel when you're trying to make a life with someone, and the other person doesn't see your spirit or care about your feelings.''

Marcy held her hands out to him, palms up. ''Lance, please don't go back to Montana and ask that woman to marry you. I know you want a home and a family. But I'm begging you to wait until you find love and someone who wants to settle down and build that home with you.''

He nearly knocked the chair over in his haste to reach her and wrap her safely in his arms. ''Honey,'' he groaned. "You told me that whole story, spilled your guts, just to keep me from making a mistake?"

Nodding her head against his chest, she melted into his embrace.

Never before had he been so amazed. Never before had anyone cared that much about him. Never.

"I…" His voice was so rough he wasn't sure he could make a coherent sentence. But he had to try. "Somewhere over the past few days, I'd already come to the conclusion that Lorna and I don't have a future together. I suppose I picked her because I wanted a family so badly and she was there. But wanting something isn't the same as making it happen…or making it right."

Marcy threw her arms around his neck and clung to him. "Thank heaven," she sighed. "Promise me you'll wait for the magic."

"I still don't believe in magic," he murmured against her ear. "But I believe in this."

He covered her mouth with his, and the atmosphere in the room suddenly changed from soft and homey to passionate and sensual. Warm turned to hot in an instant.

The kiss deepened, becoming desperate and needy as their tongues tangled and each pleaded for more. Lance covered her breast with his palm, then gently pushed her back slightly to give him access to both nipples. She felt them harden and press against the material of her bra.

Without a word they ripped at each other's clothes, and soon stood together naked and aching. He bent to take one ready and erect nipple in his mouth and a stab of pleasure went straight to her core.

Her knees wobbled so she hung on to him with both hands while he bit and laved both sensitive tips. As the heat overtook her, she trailed one hand over his hip then caressed his muscled thigh. Finally she cupped his bottom and pulled his aroused body against her belly.

Driven wild with need by the feel of him, she ran her hand between them to his groin and stroked his hard erection. The sensual and conflicting feelings of silky skin and hard scorching heat under her fingers consumed all the air in the room. She gasped.

He groaned and grabbed her shoulders. From somewhere in her dusky haze of desire, Marcy recognized that his hands were shaking as badly as hers. Pulling her to him, he lowered them to the kitchen table with his back flat on the surface and his feet still firmly planted on the floor.

Taking the golden opportunity, she explored him with her tongue. Enthralled by the pleasure he was getting from her moves, she tasted and licked her way down his body and thoroughly enjoyed the sounds of his heavy breathing.

"Enough," he groaned as he dragged her up and kissed her lips with an abandon that drove her insane. She crawled on the table and positioned her knees beside his hips, slowly fitting herself down on him.

Allowing only one inch of his tip inside her, she lifted up again and grinned to herself as he groaned, bent upward in the middle and bit her nipple. So this was what had been so missing from her world, this spell of raw need and tender teasing.

She lowered her bottom down two inches the next time, then pulled up again as he writhed below her and rubbed his callused thumbs across her peaks. "Stop," he gasped.

Laughing and completely entranced by what she could do to him, she hesitated above him and gazed into his glazed eyes. The desperation and the erotic longing were easy to see, but she also saw herself looking back and imagined a fascinating glimmer of witchcraft in her eyes.

They were surrounded by the magic. She saw it, felt it heavy in the air around them. The sizzle of it was beyond her experience, but she knew it meant trouble.

With her thighs trembling from holding back, she jammed down hard against his hips, driving him to the hilt of her desire. Lance shuddered, but let her set the pace.

While she raised then lowered her body and rubbed her breasts against his chest, he ran a hand up her spine, sending tingles to mix with the deep spicy sensations. She began to feel the tremors sneaking up on her like a thief in the night, ready to take her too far, too fast.

Trying to still, to make the pleasure last, Marcy was met instead by Lance's rage of need. He plunged upward and begged her to come with him.

A blinding rash of heat and stars captured them both as they clung to each through the earthquake of joint climax.

Laying her head on his chest, she luxuriated in the last of the spiraling jolts. But while she caught her breath and listened to his heart pound, the reality of her situation sunk in.

She'd fallen in love with him. Really, desperately and passionately in love.

If she'd imagined at the start that this would be the outcome of their time together, she would've found another way to get to Cheyenne. She wished she'd never gotten to know him. Never learned how they fit together. Even finding another job altogether would've been easier to handle than the pain she predicted was coming next.

He wrapped his arms around her. "You are absolutely perfect," he whispered.

She placed her lips against his chest then raised her hand to caress his cheek. "Not me. It's you that's so wonderful."

Lance drew them up together until they were standing in the kitchen with their arms wound around each other's waists. He tenderly kissed her lips then leaned back to gaze at her face while he smiled at her.

"You look thoroughly pleased," he grinned. "You should always look that way."

A frisson of pure panic drove through her veins as she realized what was coming next. "Lance, no…"

"Honey," he interrupted. "Why don't you and Angie come with me to Montana? We're good together. We can make a home, build a family."

The pain through her heart was as bad as she'd anticipated. If only she didn't want him, love him, almost beyond good sense. This was going to hurt him and it was the very last thing she'd wanted to do.

But he belonged on his ranch, with his friends around him. And she didn't belong there at all. He was part of nature...wild and untamed...beautiful and free. She had no idea where on earth she truly belonged, and she needed to find out before her soul completely disappeared like her mother's had so long ago.

She stepped out of his embrace and took a breath. "No, Lance. That's not a good idea."

The look of agony on his face was nearly unbearable. "We don't have anything in common," she told him softly. "This trip has been a dream and not real. Our emotions have gotten all tangled up with our bodies, but we really want different things out of life."

"Marcy...please...wait..." He looked shell-shocked, and it was all she could do not to reach for him.

She forced herself to take another step back and bent to pick up her clothes. This was hard enough to do without standing there naked before him.

"You know it's true," she said with a cracked voice. "I will always want to travel and see the world. I'd be miserable living on your ranch. And you...all you want in life is a home. A place to settle and call your own."

Stepping into her jeans, she ignored the panties and bra in favor of covering herself in a hurry. "We're like fire and water. It would be a terrible mix."

He blinked then set his jaw. "I suppose you're right." Reaching a hand to her cheek, he tenderly ran a finger along her jaw and traced her mouth as if he meant to memorize the lines. ''But we would've really set the place on fire first. We'd have gone out in a blaze of glory.''

The pain in his gut burned white-hot and with fierce intensity. On this trip, for the first time in his life, the empty loneliness that followed him everywhere had disappeared—but the agreeable feeling that replaced it had apparently only been a temporary thing.

Though he had a few more hours left to bask in Marcy and Angie's warmth, the gut-wrenching solitude he knew so well loomed ahead with a deep, cold shadow across his life.

Marcy's face contorted in sadness while she gripped her clothes and thumped a fisted hand against her breast as if her heart was breaking in two. His own heart ached just watching her pain. He wanted to make it better, easier for her somehow, but his mind was still blurred with the false promise of an end to his quest.

He didn't dare touch her again; it would lead him right back to that paradise. So he yanked on his jeans and set to work. There was a lot for them to do before every trace of their time here was erased.

With a heavy heart, he helped Marcy take down the decorations. He slipped one of the aluminum stars she'd made into his pocket when she wasn't looking. After he was home on the ranch, maybe he would make another wish on that star and start off again in search of his dream.

Lance quickly closed off the thought, because at

the moment he wasn't willing to accept all the pain he knew was heading his way. He fixed a quiet scowl upon his face, set his shoulders and finished his work. He dragged the tree outside, put the baby's crib back in the attic and cleaned.

By the time all that was done, the neighbor showed up and they dug out the SUV. The last of his few remaining hours with the two sweet females was racing by like a fireman on the way to put out a fire.

All afternoon Marcy was quiet and seemed as pensive as he felt. After they ate and cleaned up the kitchen one last time, she asked if he minded driving at night.

"I think Angie might sleep through the trip if we drive after dark," she told him. "It'll be easier on her…on all of us." Marcy's smile was bittersweet, and it cut a path right through his heart.

Lance agreed to the night trip because, now that the decision had been made and the last remnants of their time together was slipping away, he didn't think he could stand to stay here much longer and keep his hands to himself.

Every time he moved past Marcy or pulled some luggage from her hands, it took a supreme effort not to reach out for her. It was hard enough to think of letting the baby out of his sight for good.

The normal six-hour drive took closer to eight, and they arrived in Cheyenne just as daylight came creeping over the horizon from the east behind them. Thinking about the direction of the rising sun, he reminded himself to go over the Four Directions again once he was headed home...and was back to being alone.

He managed to find a fairly nice motel and paid three weeks in advance for a cozy room with a kitchenette. Marcy let him take a nap while she borrowed the SUV to make a run to the grocery store and to contact her new employers.

But soon...too soon...he found himself holding Angie in his right arm while reaching for Marcy and a last hug with the left. She didn't step into his embrace but hung back as tears welled in her eyes.

Lifting her face with his free hand, he bent and touched her lips with his own in an achingly tender kiss. He wanted to savor it and keep the memory with him for his darkest hours.

Angie cried and put her arms around his neck. "No."

Marcy pulled back. "She doesn't want you to go."

He didn't want to go, either. But it was time. So he handed the baby over and gave Marcy his business card, telling her to contact him if she ever needed his help.

Then he turned his back on them...and walked away from everything that had ever really mattered.

Eleven

He cursed himself for letting his dreams overtake his reality. Slamming the SUV's door, he jammed it into gear and took off for home. Dazed and hurting, he headed for the interstate and set the cruise control.

Needing to think through his life—to get *himself* back under cruise control—Lance didn't pay much attention to the road. He'd traveled it so many times in the past, anyway. Instead, he desperately tried to calm down and find a way past the awful pain.

He rubbed at a place on his chest, right above his heart. How could just leaving them behind hurt so much?

It was a deep physical pain, worse than any he could remember. The time that crazy bull stepped on his back and broke three ribs had been bad. But not this bad.

And some of the things he'd put himself through on the rez, those things he thought would prove that he was a man, none of those had ever been this painful. But he just couldn't get a grip on why.

Why was this different?

Perhaps...because he was being selfish. Though not particularly pleasant, he figured that thought was something to be considered. For as long as he could remember, when he let himself want something—when he let himself hope—the results were always the same.

Had he totally ignored what Marcy wanted in his zeal to grab a new bright life? He tried to focus on the things that she had told him.

"Soul loneliness" she'd called it. He couldn't entirely understand what she meant. Swallowing back a fuzzy lump in his throat, he kept going over her words. She'd wanted him to have his home and his family—but with someone else.

Why? Why not with her and Angie?

Suddenly it hit him, like a damned cartoon lightbulb going on over his head. Of course. A home to Marcy was someplace bad. Someplace where things hurt you instead of a place where there were good vibrations and people who cared—the way *he'd* always dreamed.

What an idiot he'd been. He'd done the exact thing she'd tried to warn him against. He hadn't paid a bit of attention to her spirit or her feelings.

"Marcy..." he groaned to himself. "I was such a fool. I didn't really listen to you."

She was absolutely right. They didn't belong together. Lance wasn't positive at the moment that he belonged with anyone. He'd been a selfish bastard and had gotten just what he deserved.

Marcy finished changing Angie and set her down on the motel room floor so she could crawl around. "Okay, Ange, play for a while and release some of that energy. Your mama is miserable. I'm afraid I'm not going to be much fun tonight."

Angie plopped her bottom on the rug and pointed up to her. "Ma-ma."

The surprising tears came fast and furious, leaving Marcy with a lump in her throat and a pain in her chest so bad it almost doubled her over. "Oh, Angie," she sobbed. "Mama is such a jerk. You're starting to talk…starting to do such wonderful things… and we don't have anyone to share that with. I sent away the only one who cared."

"Ba!"

"Yes…yes. He gave you Baby," Marcy reached for the doll and handed it to her child. "There you go, sweetheart. You have your Baby even if you don't have the daddy you need. Your mama was too afraid to grab a good thing when she saw it."

Marcy sat on the edge of the bed. "Oh God, what have I done?" She swiped at the tears and leaned her face into her palms. "I was so scared. So afraid to take a chance."

"Da."

Though her eyes were blurred with tears, Marcy glanced down at Angie and smiled sadly. "Da… Yes, baby, he could've been your daddy. He wanted it, and

I'm sure he loves you. It was just *me* that he wasn't too sure about.''

She closed her eyes and longed for the feel of Lance's arms around her…his lips on hers…his hands on her body. More than merely awakening her body, his intensity had touched her very soul and brought her back to life.

And she'd refused to go home with him. Somebody should come commit her; she'd totally lost her sanity.

"I wanted him to feel the magic," she told Angie. "I needed him to love me the same way I love him."

"Da."

"Yes. I want him, too, Ange. I want him so badly my whole body aches." She bent and picked up her child, hugging her to her breast. "But we can't make someone love us, no matter how much we might want them to."

Rocking Angie back and forth, Marcy buried her face in her baby's sweet-smelling hair. "I love you, Ange. And I'll always be here for you, I promise. I won't marry someone who doesn't love me, and end up giving you the kind of life my mother gave me."

Angie started to whimper, picking up on her mother's sad mood.

"But I love him so much," Marcy cried. She didn't want Angie to be unhappy, but it was too hard for her to stay strong.

At least she had Angie, she thought. They had each other…and they always would.

With a startled gasp, Marcy suddenly realized what she'd really done. She drew Angie back and looked down at her daughter through blurred eyes. "Angie, we have each other. But he's all alone."

She tried to blink back the tears. "I can't believe I've been so selfish. He did everything in his power to take care of us and make us happy, and he didn't deserve to be turned away like that. What was I thinking?"

The baby started to cry, and her mother tried to give her some comfort by patting her back. But Marcy's own tears were running freely down her cheeks. "I hurt the man I love more than life. Why couldn't I see that before it was too late?"

Angie threw her arms around her mother's neck and shrieked. "All right, sweetheart." Marcy tried to soothe her. "I'll try, but I don't know if I can make it right. The damage might be too big, the pain too strong. But I love him enough to take the risk."

Driving on, Lance was only vaguely aware of his surroundings. He barely noticed when the sun made its final descent and left the gray, lifeless sky behind for the rest of the day. The darkness that came after sunset could not possibly match the black, yawning hole inside him.

What could he do in order to go on from here? The ranch in Montana didn't seem to hold the same cozy, homey spot in his heart that it had only a few days ago. Without Marcy and Angie, no place held a lot of appeal.

He couldn't think clearly, so he kept on heading home. There were things in Montana he needed to do.

People who were counting on him. Meeting his responsibilities was all that was left to him.

Always in the past when he'd been lost and without direction, the lessons he'd learned from the Dine had served him well. That was where he'd first learned about the importance of family. To the Navajo, nothing is more important than family.

He'd wanted so badly to fit in on the rez, to be worthy of being included in the family. But he never truly belonged with them. Just as he had never truly belonged in Grandmother Steele's world, either.

Joining the rodeo circuit and traveling the country had been only a means of searching for a place where he belonged. And he'd been so sure that place was the Montana ranch and the Stanton family who lived there.

Now...

Now, he just didn't know how to find his direction. Wanting to seek a center, to stabilize and balance his life as he had on the back of a horse, Lance decided to review aloud the Four Directions in Navajo Life one more time.

"East is the direction of the dawn and is the thinking direction." He'd probably missed that direction when he'd jumped in and asked Marcy to come to Montana with him.

"South...that's the planning direction. The direction where I should've planned my actions after thinking them through." With a roll of his eyes, he continued. "West, the direction of home. West is a Navajo's life, the place where they do their living as they act out their plan and their thoughts."

After he arrived at home he could look to the North. "The direction where a Navajo finds satisfaction and can evaluate the outcome of what was first started in the east," he quoted from his old lessons.

The Dine believe that when a person falls, they must stand back up and see what they can do differently the next day. At this moment Lance figured he might never be able to crawl back up again.

Thinking back to his original indecision about going to New Orleans for Grandmother Steele's funeral and how surprised he'd been to find that she'd had other family members he'd never known, Lance tried to see his mistakes.

Lucille Steele had had several children, nieces and nephews. New aunts, uncles and cousins that he'd had never even heard of before. He didn't hang around long enough to find out what they thought of having a half-breed relative.

Learning about all that extended family had been quite a shock. He'd ambled around in a hazy fog of amazement over the drastic changes to his ideas of family, until he'd bumped into the old gypsy woman. And she had been an amazement all on her own.

But was this crazy trip he was on about finding his extended family and then wanting his own home so badly he could taste it? Or was it something more? It made him wonder if that gypsy had put some sort of spell on him.

Lance pulled over to a rest stop and dug in his pocket for the ring. Getting the ring had started everything.

He rubbed his fingers over the velvet box, expecting to feel a static charge as he had when he'd shown Marcy the ring. But nothing happened.

Tearing open the box, Lance stared down at the empty space in shock. He was sure he hadn't ever removed the ring from its box. So where was it?

Dammit. Losing Marcy and Angie was bad enough. Had he also managed to lose the ring?

He furiously swiped a hand across his eyes and fought the pain. Lost…alone.

Blindly starting up the SUV and driving toward home, Lance vowed to rethink his entire life before he ever made another stupid move like this one.

As the night began to give way to the gray cast of morning, Lance finally looked up to see where he was. But he was having trouble getting his bearings.

Then he saw the craggy peaks of the Badlands out of the windshield and had to pull over to catch his breath. All this time he hadn't been driving toward home in Montana at all. He'd driven himself right back to where he'd started the day before yesterday, Bobby and Vicki's ranch house.

Oh, man. Talk about not thinking and planning before you act. Jeez, this was the absolute height of spontaneity…and stupidity.

He needed to turn around and head west, back to his Montana home. But he was tired now, and maybe he should rest first.

Lance wouldn't allow himself to think that he'd come all the way back here because this was the first place that he'd ever really felt at home. That thought did niggle at the back of his mind, but he refused to let it in.

Instead he drove down the plowed and cleared roads that a few days ago had been treacherous and covered in ice. Bobby and Vicki's place had been a magical white wonderland then. Today, everything looked a little brown around the edges and terribly ordinary, just a typical winter day in South Dakota farmland.

As he neared the ranch house, Lance spotted smoke coming from the chimney of Bobby and Vicki's house. Half a mile closer and he saw Bobby's big four-door truck in front of the house. The family had come home early from their Florida holiday.

Well, he supposed they wouldn't mind if he stopped in and rested for a while. It would be really good to see them again after so long.

Later, after calling Montana to check on his employees, then taking a nap and eating a huge dinner meal with the family, Lance trudged outside with Bobby to cut more firewood.

"I'm glad you showed up today, Steele," Bobby teased. "You and your guests burned most of the wood I'd set aside. Now you get to replace it."

Lance hefted the long-handled ax in his fist and grunted. "Should've done it before we left. But I wasn't thinking."

Bobby chuckled at his friend. "Yeah. And you're doing such a better job of thinking now, aren't you?"

"Huh?" Lance narrowed an eye at his buddy and saw the sly grin. "How come you guys came back early?" he asked in the hopes of changing the subject.

"Vicki and the kids didn't think it felt right to spend Christmas in Florida," Bobby admitted. "No snowmen. No seeing your breath hanging on the air. No white Christmas. It just wasn't the same.''

"Right. They missed one of the whitest Christmases on record around here,'' Lance grumbled.

"So we heard.'' Bobby stopped walking and stood by the cord of wood he'd stacked earlier in the fall. "Actually, I think everyone was homesick. It just wasn't the same without all the family around.''

Lance picked up a piece of wood and set it up for splitting. "Christmas Eve was nice here. Thanks for the use of the house. Sorry you missed it.''

Bobby stopped the first swing by clamping a hand on his friend's shoulder. "You look terrible, bud. If everything is so great, why do you look so miserable?''

Lance didn't respond or look over at Bobby. He just jerked his shoulder back and raised his arms to complete the swing.

As he split the wood with a crack, Lance thought of how wonderful Bobby and Vicki's house had looked on Christmas Eve and Christmas morning. When he'd first gone back inside this morning, he'd been terribly disappointed that even the smell wasn't the same. But he didn't know how to say that to his friend—so he stayed silent.

Bobby crossed his arms over his chest and watched him split a few more logs. "Marianne told Vicki that you were pretty hung up on the woman you brought here. Marcy…right?''

Lance wiped his brow against his shoulder then shrugged. He wasn't sure if "hung up'' really said it all.

"Oh, man," Bobby laughed as he looked him in the eyes. "You're a goner. Just imagine, White Eagle Steele miserable over a woman after all these years of being fancy-free."

Lance grunted again, then scowled over at his old friend. "Shut up, Bobby. I should be back in Montana right now. I'm a little put out that I got twisted around, that's all there is to it. Don't make a big thing."

Taking the ax from his hands, Bobby grinned at him. "Grab some logs. It's getting colder out here."

Lance filled his arms with split logs, and the two of them headed back toward the house. "It was kinda strange, though," he said as they walked. "I was thinking so hard about going home. But when I looked up, I'd come here instead of heading back to Montana."

"Hmm. And what do you think now?"

"I don't know. I guess I was thinking that your place felt like home, but now…" He hesitated and glanced over at his friend. "No offense, but it doesn't feel like home."

Bobby laughed. "No offense taken, pal. I wasn't prepared to invite you to live with us, anyway."

They arrived at the house and dropped their loads of wood on the ground. "You know," Bobby added as he bent to stack the logs next to the house. "Maybe it's not the place you're thinking of as home but the woman. I know that if Vicki decided she had to live on Mars, that would be where I felt at home. Wherever she is…that's home for me."

Lance froze where he stood. Was that it? Was that the truth he'd been trying to get his head around?

He blinked a couple of times, exhaled slowly and then helped Bobby stack the wood. Maybe…before he made another huge mistake…he ought to talk it all out with Bobby. Just maybe, this time, he'd do the Four Directions in their proper order.

The ache in his chest began loosening its fierce grip around his heart. He would take his time in the telling, make sure he didn't leave out any of the details of the past ten days.

He stuck his hands in his pockets, trying to decide how to start. When his fingers touched a tinfoil star, Lance remembered—everything important.

Talk. Think. Plan. Live.

North, east, south and west. Maybe the place wasn't nearly as important as the direction.

"Just another block, Angie," Marcy told her daughter.

She felt the baby shivering in her arms. Opening the front of her heavy parka, Marcy hugged her child tightly to her chest, wrapped her coat around both of them and held them secure together against the elements.

"It will be okay." She sniffed back the tears that threatened to swamp her. "We'll find him somehow. I promise." She couldn't cry right now, both for her baby's sake and because the tears would probably freeze right to her cheeks.

The snow had begun to come down several blocks

ago. Now it fell in huge, wet clumps, slowing her progress and leaving her chilled to the bone.

"Some day you're going to love the snow, Ange. I'll show you how to build a snowman and snow angels…and we'll even slide down the hill on a sled." Just as the words slipped off her tongue, she found herself thinking of how much nicer it would be if Lance could've shown Angie all those things. The tears threatened once more and she fought them off with the back of her hand across her eyes.

As falling snow further obscured her vision, Marcy wondered if she'd been careless and stupid to bring her child out in this weather. But she hadn't taken the time to think it all the way through when she'd made the decision to find a phone and then head on to the bus terminal to check out the schedules.

He wasn't home yet. It took a bit of doing to round up the change she needed for the call, but she'd dealt with it eventually. She called the number from the card he'd given her, but no one answered.

Where was he? She shivered, not from the cold, but from the thought that he was out there somewhere all alone. He'd looked so miserable when he left. The pain of remembering it sliced through her heart all over again.

She looked up and realized they were nearing the motel. "Almost there, Ange. Just another few feet."

Through the blowing snowflakes, Marcy saw a hulking figure silhouetted against the door to their motel room. The first spit of panic quickly gave way to a tiny breath of hope. The figure was hunched against the cold and hard to make out. But another step and she caught the unmistakable sight of a cowboy hat pulled low over his eyes.

Lance. Thank God.

"Lance…" She tried to call his name, but the emotions were clogging her throat and the word came out more like a squeak.

But it was enough. He straightened and turned.

There. The word drove through him. *There at last is my heart.*

He scrambled to reach them. "Marcy…Angie…" He pulled her to him and wrapped them in his embrace.

Marcy drew the key from her pocket and handed it over. Dragging them all inside and closing the door behind him, Lance took another minute to hold them both against his chest. To let the feel of these two sweet females alive and safe pulse through his body and give him back his heartbeat.

The room was warm, and within a few seconds he helped her off with her coat. Then he pulled off his hat and coat and waited, not particularly patiently, for her to get Angie out of the snowsuit.

Once she had the baby warmed and sleeping quietly on the bed between two stacks of pillows, she turned. "I…"

Grabbing her, he slanted a rough kiss across her tender mouth. She stiffened at the surprise move, then melted against him and twined her arms around his neck. She parted her lips, and their tongues tangled in a demanding and possessive taste of heaven.

He could've stood there all day, maybe forever,

holding her this way. But reluctantly he lifted his head and looked down into dazed eyes.

"That was…well…I just had to do that before anything else," he mumbled.

He felt her tremble and wasn't sure he was strong enough to keep them both upright. Taking her arm, he helped her over to the tiny kitchenette table, pulled out a chair and waited for her to sit.

"Marcy, where were…" He shook his head and turned to pace the little room. "No. Never mind. That's not what I want to talk about first." If he didn't get all this off his chest right now, he was sorely afraid he would explode.

"Lance…"

Waving her into silence, he opened his mouth again. "Just listen for a second." Now that it was time to say his piece he felt nervous, wondering if the words he used would be good enough…good enough to make a difference.

"All my life I dreamed of a home…a place where I would be wanted. I needed someone to care, to see the real me. I wanted it so badly that…well, I got the place and the caring all mixed up in my head." He took a breath and paced over to check on Angie.

The baby's eyes were still closed, but she seemed to be stirring. He wanted to get this all said before Angie woke up and needed attention. Jerking around to face Marcy, he stopped, stunned as that beautiful face came into view.

She stared up at him blankly. But she had the most exquisite…the most gorgeous face in the universe. He swallowed back the lump that formed in his chest and moved to his throat.

Needing desperately to find a way to get through to her, Lance rushed ahead. ''When you talked of caring about someone's spirit and feelings, I still didn't get it. I thought my heart's desire was for a home and family. But it turns out that caring about someone…having someone care about me…is what I wished for all along.''

''Oh, Lance.'' She started to get up, but he gently pushed her back down.

He wasn't done yet. She still wasn't smiling at him, and he just had to make her see—see his spirit.

''I think, at least I hope, that you do care for me, Marcy. And I know you and Angie mean everything to me.'' He gulped air into his lungs and continued past whatever it was that suddenly blurred his vision. ''I don't need a home. All I need are you two. I can't…''

He fisted his hands and set his jaw. ''I won't…live without you.'' Steadying himself, he continued. ''I plan to give up my job at the ranch. I'll take you anywhere. I'd really like an opportunity to show you the world. 'Cause, wherever you want to go…that's where I want to be.''

The tears streamed down her face and drove that horrible ache into his chest again. ''Please, Marcy, say you'll marry me. Don't make me have to trail behind you and Angie while you travel all over the earth.''

He reached for her then, pulled her up and tenderly

wiped his thumbs under her eyes to stem the flow of tears. "You are my heart...my soul.

"I've never been in love before so I wasn't too sure how this should go." He cradled her precious face in his hands. "I planned on giving you the gypsy's ring because you are definitely my heart's desire. Except, when I wanted to look at it, the ring was gone. Lost."

Miracle of miracles, she looked up into his eyes and smiled. "L-love? You love me." The last was said not as a question but as a softly whispered prayer.

He answered her the only way he knew how, with a kiss that put his whole spirit...his whole life on the line.

"I love you, too," she said as she nibbled on his bottom lip. "With everything I am. And, ring or not, I will marry you."

Pulling back to stare at her, he felt the grin spreading across his face. Speechless, he could only hold her tight and smile.

"Ba!" Angie's shout brought them both up.

Marcy took his hand and went to her daughter's side. "All right, Ange. Here's your baby." She bent and picked up the doll he'd given the little girl for Christmas.

Angie buried her face in the doll's hair and it was more than he could stand. He dragged both the sweet child and her doll into his arms. "Oh, Angie. I forgot I had someone else to ask. Will you marry me, too?"

"Lance, look." Marcy was pointing at the bed.

There, sitting atop the bedspread at the spot where

Angie had been, was the gypsy's ring. For a moment he was too stunned to move.

The air sizzled. And the magic settled in around them.

He transferred Angie to one arm and picked up the ring. Putting it on Marcy's finger, he thought his heart would burst with happiness…and wonder.

"Marcy, the gypsy told me to let this ring lead me to my heart's desire. I guess it was always meant for you." Pulling her close, he continued. "I know it brought us together. You and Angie made me believe."

He sighed and hugged them both tighter. "And I swear to you, for as long as I live, I will always see your spirit and believe in the magic."

Epilogue

The twinkling lights along the Seine lit up the crisp, Parisian air, reminding her it was almost Christmas. Marcy tightened her grip on Angie's hand and waited for the toddler to catch up.

Lance stopped beside them and put his arm around her shoulder. "Are you getting cold, honey? I could hail a cab. We don't want to be late for Christmas Eve dinner."

She shook her head and smiled up at her beloved husband. "Angie needs the exercise. There's time and we're not too cold." At least, not like last Christmas, she thought.

"You sure you don't want Daddy to carry you, baby girl?" he coaxed Angie.

"Daddy, me," the baby said as she lifted her arms. He bent and swung her up, stabilizing the precious load on his right forearm. Angie clung to him, giggling.

Lance looked so tall and broad, so spectacular in his black winter dress coat with his hair slicked back in a black thong. Her baby had on a new red velvet coat, with her hair pulled up under a soft white fur bonnet. They made quite a picture, these two strings to her soul.

Marcy's heart shifted, as it did every time she saw the two of them together. It was so hard sometimes to remember that this wonderful child, this strong and handsome man, this whole fabulous life somehow really belonged to her.

"Lance, can we go home tomorrow?" she asked.

He turned to her and slipped his arm around her waist. "Back to Montana? On Christmas Day?"

"Well, okay, maybe not. But the day after tomorrow?"

He gave her a quizzical smile. "But I thought we were going to spend Christmas here, then stop in to see Venice before we headed back this time."

She snuggled into his embrace. "I'm homesick. I miss our house, our friends...the snow." Laughing at her own sentimentality, she beamed up at her dear husband. "I know it's easiest for you to travel over the holidays when not much is happening on the ranch. But I'd rather be at home."

Lance chuckled. "Okay, my world traveler. Whatever you want."

"I have a present for you, and I wanted to wait until we got home to give it to you," she told him. "But...I can't wait."

He stopped and tilted his head to look down at her. "Okay. Is it back at the hotel?"

"No." She placed her hand against her belly, already protecting the life that grew there. "It's right here. It's our new…well…either boy or girl. Does it matter to you which?"

Lance stared at her for a startled minute, then quickly swung her up against him again and danced them all around in a circle. "Boy or girl? Wow. Who cares? Another baby is fantastic." He laughed, and Angie shrieked.

"Yes, let's go home, little mother," he said after he kissed her. "I've only got a few months to spoil you rotten and I need to get started right away."

The warmth filled Marcy with every good feeling she had ever longed to have. It was good to be the queen of a growing and happy family.

But it was much better, in the end, to let yourself believe in the *magic*.

*   *   *   *   *